I0557541

Also by Ev Bishop

Bigger Things
A Sharla Brown Christmas
Wedding Bands (River's Sigh B & B, Book 1)
Hooked (River's Sigh B & B, Book 2)
Spoons (River's Sigh B & B, Book 3)
Hook, Line & Sinker (River's Sigh B & B, Book 4)
Silver Bells
(A River's Sigh B & B Christmas novella, Book 5)
Reeling (River's Sigh B & B, Book 6)
New Year's Resolution: One To Keep
(A River's Sigh B & B novella, Book 7)
The Catch (River's Sigh B & B, Book 8)

Writing as Toni Sheridan
The Present
Drummer Boy

EV BISHOP

New Year's Resolution: One to Keep

River's Sigh B & B, Book 7

New Year's Resolution: ONE TO KEEP
Book 7 in the River's Sigh B & B series
Copyright © 2020 Ev Bishop

Print Edition

Published by Winding Path Books

ISBN 978-1-77265-044-0

Cover image: Kimberly Killion / The Killion Group Inc.

All rights reserved. Except for brief quotations used in critical articles or reviews, the reproduction or use of this work in whole or in part in any form, now known or hereafter invented, is forbidden without the written permission of the publisher, Winding Path Books, 1886 Creek St., Terrace, British Columbia, V8G 4Y1, Canada.

New Year's Resolution: ONE TO KEEP is a work of fiction. Names, characters, places, and incidents are either the product of the author's imagination or are used fictitiously, and any resemblance to actual persons, living or dead, business establishments, events or locales is entirely coincidental.

For TC and Margie,

Oh, how I love you two! I am very grateful to have you in my life. Thank you for everything.

Chapter 1

Boxing Day

THE MULLED WINE SOPHIE WAS drinking, advertised as the pub's "Festive Favorite," was sweet, spicy and deliciously warming. The two mugs she'd already enjoyed called for a third. She lifted her empty glass and nodded, smiling when the sweet-faced server, a woman around her age, saw her and called from across the room, "Another, miss?"

Miss. It had been a while since anyone called her miss. She was getting ma'am a lot. It was terrible. She didn't feel like a ma'am. She definitely felt like a miss. Definitely. She grinned to herself, knowing she was getting silly on the wine and liking it. See, this was the life—eat what you want, drink what you want, take off on a spontaneous trip whenever you want. People often asked her, "Doesn't it get lonely?"

Truthfully—and only to herself and even then usually only after a few drinks—yes, it did sometimes. But as she was always lecturing her younger sister, Kate, a hopeless romantic, married to her high school sweet-

1

heart, raising three kids and a zoo of various pets, "It's better to be alone and to be lonely sometimes than to be with someone and truly alone." Besides she had books. Who needed a flesh and blood man when there were books? Okay, she hadn't really fallen that far. She could definitely think of a few occasions where flesh and blood guys were beyond lovely, but she was sitting in an empty bar the day after Christmas in a completely foreign-to-her small town. Thinking of some of the physical qualities of the male gender would only be frustrating—and she was giving up men. It was part of her new flying solo thing. Sex, for her at least, always came with emotional entanglements. Emotional entanglements always led to pain. She was done with it. She would have true love or nothing, and since she didn't believe in true love anymore, nothing it was.

Her wine arrived, all cinnamon, clove and orangey smelling. Mmm! And just in the nick of time. She'd almost fallen into her least favorite, most predictable thought groove, and she was determined to avoid that sinkhole. She was not only going to commit to a single life by choice, she was going to delight in it and live each day with joy and abundant gratitude. (Wow, was this really only her third drink? With a gloopy, overly sentimental moment like that, it felt like much more.)

The waitress saved her from her inner monologue again. "Would you like to order something to eat?"

"Oh, yes. Thanks." Sophie had perused the surpris-

2

ingly enticing menu at length. "I'll have the Sunday carve, please. Rare, if possible."

"Good choice. It's fantastic. Would you like a starter too?"

"Um, no. There's a dessert I've got my eye on, and I'll be having more wine. I have lots of room, but it's not unlimited." Sophie patted her stomach at the last line and the server laughed.

"Good choice, times two. Every single one of our desserts is unbelievable. Our dessert menu was created by a local chef, Callum Archer—"

"Callum Archer? Get out of town! As in River's Sigh B & B Callum Archer?"

The server nodded.

"That's where I'm staying this week. Well, I'm in town tonight, but I check in tomorrow."

"You'll love it, but wait . . . I thought Jo and Callum were closing for a week and heading out of town 'til after New Year's. Are you sure you have the dates right?"

Sophie loved this small town banter thing. People shared information so casually here. "Yeah, but after seeing the pictures, I begged, and they said they have a caretaker, so as long as I didn't mind breakfast being a simple affair and being the only paying guest, I was good to go."

"You'll totally love it," the server enthused once more, and Sophie found it refreshing. It was nice to meet someone else who didn't mind being unabashedly

3

enthusiastic. While there probably was a limit to how truly great every one of her choices could be or how much she'd "totally love" something, the woman didn't have that going-through-the-motions, sell-sell-sell tone service industry workers sometimes adopt for survival. She seemed to mean her words.

"What's your name, by the way?" Sophie asked as the woman was about to leave.

"Stella."

"Nice to meet you, Stella." Sophie repeated the name so it would stick in her brain and held out a hand for Stella to shake. "I'm Sophie."

"Nice to meet you too, Sophie. I hope you enjoy your time in Greenridge."

"So far so good."

Stella smiled, promised her dinner would be along shortly, and called out greetings to a group of four and a tagalong guy who banged through the pub's front door. A dusting of sugar-crisp snow and a gust of cold wind traipsed in with them.

Sophie turned back to the book she'd been reading, anticipation and contentment rolling through her. It was good so far. The perfect story for a deep winter night. She'd been right to make this impromptu escape. Christmas had been a gloomy excuse for everyone in her life to comment on what she didn't have or to ask with big, wide-eyed shows of concern, "How are you doing? No, seriously, *how are you*?"

It made her nuts. It had been two years since Kyle

jilted her at the altar. Get over it, people! She had. Or pretty much anyway. The hardest part these days was accepting the fact that he'd been right. That he'd done her a favor. Once she'd gotten over the worst of the pain, she'd been able to see that. It just would've been nice if he could've done it before they forked out all that money and perhaps not with every single one of their nearest and dearest watching on. He'd realized that she wouldn't change and that as she was, they weren't compatible.

What she didn't understand was why wanting to travel alone occasionally, wanting to continue doing silly things just because they were fun, loving to read and play pretend—yes, even at the ancient age of twenty-eight—were such deal breakers. She thought her financial independence, the fact that she had a life and didn't need or want to be with some guy 24/7, and her sitting on the fence about whether she wanted to have kids or not were personality strengths. Kyle didn't.

"You don't need me," Kyle had said. "You don't need anyone."

"Why do I have to need you? Why can't I just want you? Why can't we just want each other? Why can't that be enough?" It was their oldest argument, and he never had a satisfying answer.

He also didn't like that she carried a few extra pounds—didn't understand why she ate carbs and didn't go to the gym like all the women from his firm.

She didn't know why she even had to explain. "Because I love food, I love cooking." And good grief, she was healthy and fit. Besides, you just had to look at her family. "We're strong peasant stock," she said. "Made for hard work, loving and baby making."

Kyle never found that comment funny, either. "You don't even want to change. You're fine just being what you are."

So that's what it came down to, wasn't it? He couldn't stand that she A) didn't need him, and B) didn't feel hugely motivated to change everything about herself to fit someone else's ideal.

"What about you? You eat carbs."

"It's different. I'm a guy."

She'd dated a few times since she and Kyle imploded, but her heart wasn't in it.

Sophie had often continued the argument with her sister. "It's like I have to be broken or completely unable to survive on my own for someone to think I'm worth marrying."

"You just haven't met the right guy yet," her sister Kate would always say. "Besides, being with someone requires compromise."

Sophie had no problem with that quality—practiced it in her everyday life, tried to encourage it in her classroom—but she didn't think compromise should mean sacrificing the parts of your personality that make you *you.*

So yeah, long story short, Kyle had done her a big

fat favor. *Thank you, Kyle.*

And she didn't begrudge her friends and family their spouses and children and miscellaneous other relationships. Of course she didn't. But she hadn't been able to stomach the idea of New Year's Eve just the same. No, a week of holidaying in this postcard-pretty little town was the perfect bit of pampering and celebration she needed, and the perfect segue way into her New Year's Resolution. She sipped her wine, toasted herself mentally—*Here's to you, your healed heart, and your exciting bachelorette status!*—and slipped back into the pages of her unfolding story.

Chapter 2

JESSE STOMPED THE SNOW OFF his boots on the Christmas-print doormat and inhaled the steamy, hoppy air. Warm comfort wrapped around him like a blanket. It was pretty sad when a bar felt more like home than your house did—but ah, well. Take what you can get, right? And anyway, it wasn't like he spent every night getting shit-faced. He mostly just people watched or read. Or drowned in morose thoughts, but he wasn't going there tonight. Or not this moment anyway.

"Hey, Jesse. What'll it be? The usual?" Stella—the patron saint of lost souls, or his at least—appeared at his side.

Jesse barely nodded and the pint was on the table in front of him. He'd switch to gin and tonic later, but he liked to start with beer.

"You eating?"

"Not sure."

"You should eat. You need to put food in that skinny gullet of yours."

"I already have a mother, Stella. And a sister. Back off, okay?"

"And did you go to either of their houses and eat yesterday?"

"It was Christmas."

Stella waited. He sighed explosively. Sometimes this small town bullshit was hard to take. Crystal had been right about that, at least.

He made a conscious effort not to take out his piss poor mood on Stella. Annoying as she was, she was one of the good ones. "I not only had Christmas dinner, I slept over Christmas Eve so I could take my niece and nephews sledding. In the morning—don't have a heart attack now—I was in charge of Christmas breakfast. We had it all: bacon and eggs, fresh fruit with a yogurt dip, waffles with whipped cream and warmed syrup. We played board games all afternoon until dinner. I wasn't back at my place 'til after ten."

Stella glanced toward the noisy table of four that had come in the same time he did. They were still reading their menus, and she sank into the chair across from Jesse. "And did you enjoy any of it?"

Leave it to Stella. She always found the one chink in a guy's armor. "It wasn't terrible. And being surrounded by the kids was really fun." The news was as shocking to him as it was to her. So that's how long it took for the worst of a wound to crust over. Three years. He raked his mind for the normally ever-present residual bitterness, but mostly just felt tired about the idea of giving more mental energy to his ex-wife. He didn't feel like hopping on the merry-go-round of what

9

ifs and regrets, even though it was Christmas time, his personal season for depressing reflection. Hmm, very interesting. So the injury was not only healing; he was apparently beating the worst of the infection.

Stella poked him. He jumped. "Oh, sorry, what were you saying?"

"You're hopeless." She shook her head. "But I'm glad you had a nice time. You deserve it. And I know people keep pissing you off with similar comments, but it's true. Things will keep getting better, and you'll find love again one day. Real love. Love that laughs."

Jesse swilled half his beer, burped, and wiped his mouth with his hand. Stella slapped him. "Gross."

"Not interested in wuv, wuv, twoo wuv anymore, Stel. Don't think I even believe in it."

She grunted her disagreement, but he held up a hand to stave off her rebuttal. "But getting laid? That's another thing altogether. It's been a long time. Who's the hottie?"

Stella looked irritated and confused. Her gaze darted past the still-chatting group of four and lit on the only other occupied table. "Are you talking about Sophie? Seriously? Don't be mean." Her frown deepened. "And leave her alone. She's nice."

Jesse chuckled and took another long pull from his drink. "Maybe I will, maybe I won't. Maybe I'm planning to forsake the error of my old monogamous ways and become a womanizer."

"Shut up."

Jesse shrugged. "Why not? No one ever truly knows another person, so why try? Better to be the heart breaker than the breakee, right?"

Stella opened her mouth, then shut it and smacked him again. "Okay, okay, you got me." She pushed up from the table. "Looks like the gabbers are ready. I'll bring you a G and T and a menu after I take their order."

Alone with his thoughts once more, Jesse nursed his remaining beer, flagged Stella down for another, and watched the room. A rigid, angry-looking couple entered, and then a couple of lone wolves like himself—ha ha, he liked how he made it sound cool, not lame. Guess he was done having to fend off guilt-ridden Stella for the night; she was going to be busy. Apparently he wasn't the only guy in town who needed a family-free moment and a drink or two the day after Christmas. In all seriousness though, he hoped Stella got over it someday. Yes, Crystal was her cousin and she'd introduced them. No, it wasn't her fault that Crystal played him, the furthest thing from it, actually—as he'd told her countless times. He'd been intentionally blind and stupid.

Stella breezed by his table, and he handed off his second empty pint glass and took the proffered menu and gin. As he sipped and contemplated what to eat, he had to fight not to stare at her—her being the "hottie" he'd mentioned to Stella. *Sophie.* Even the name drew him in, all soft and comfy sounding. Why had Stella

11

assumed he was being mean and been so put off by his joke? At first, he'd only referred to her because she was the solitary single female in the bar, but she was pretty. Very pretty. With sleek dark hair, ivory-cream skin and deep red lips, she reminded him of a slightly chubby Snow White. He liked her low-necked sweater too.

She was absorbed in an e-reader, and every so often a private smile put a cute dimple in her left cheek. He thought of the book he had in his jacket pocket and wanted to go over and strike up a conversation. How bizarre. First having a decent time at Christmas. Now wanting to talk to a strange female. Maybe Christmas miracles really were a thing.

He laughed at his own joke and forced himself to look away from Sophie, focusing again on the outrage his womanizing comment triggered in Stella. Seriously, what was with her? It wasn't like she had to worry. He wasn't a light fling guy, more's the pity—and he wouldn't risk the pain Crystal had caused him ever again. Besides, lots of guys lived alone and were totally fine. Hell, he'd been on his own for three years now, almost exactly, and he was all right. That settled it. Done. He'd been thinking on this resolution for the New Year for some time, and he was glad to have it reaffirmed.

To perpetual bachelorhood and leaving the toilet seat up forever! He lifted his glass in a silent toast, about to take a slug of the lemony-icy goodness—at exactly the same instant Sophie, his ivory skinned, rose-lipped stranger, happened to look up.

Her eyebrows lifted and she glanced over her shoulder both ways, then shook her head apologetically, her brow furrowing and her burgundy mouth curving in a most attractive way. She'd obviously misunderstood his toasting gesture entirely—and apparently wanted to make it clear she wasn't interested. Shit. He looked like a complete putz. He wasn't that guy who sits in a bar ogling women and hitting on them from across the room. Okay, actually, tonight he was . . . but not that way. Not like a creep. Or at least not like a complete creep. He'd go and let her know that, put her mind at ease. . . .

Chapter 3

THE BEARDED GUY WAS COMING over, drink in hand. Why? Sophie craned her neck over her shoulder again. There had to be someone at a table behind her that she hadn't noticed. Why else would he head her way? The bathrooms were in the other direction. And she was reading a book, minding her own business, sending out leave me alone signals. She'd only raised her eyes to stretch—not to be hit on by some weirdo, cute or not.

As he got closer, however, she felt every ounce of the mulled wine that muddled her thoughts and triggered a blood-surging observation. "Cute" didn't even begin to cut it. The guy was a hunk.

You're off guys, she reminded herself. And you're going to be off booze too if you can't keep a better grip on yourself when you drink.

"I'm really sorry," he said. His voice was a low, sexy tenor that fit his lean, long-legged good looks perfectly. She couldn't have picked a better voice actually. Omigod, her inner self intoned, how drunk are you?

Sexy voice leaned on her table. No doubt he'd had

14

a couple drinks too. "I wasn't hitting on you," he explained.

Oh. Well, that was a relief, right? Yes. A big . . . relief.

"I really wasn't. You don't have to worry. I don't find you attractive."

Ouch. Even drunk—yep, she admitted it, she was kind of hammered, okay, totally hammered—that didn't feel good. Maybe she actually flinched, because the guy's eyes—very nice too, sort of a whiskey colored amber—widened.

"Shit! I mean . . . well, that's not what I meant. You're fine looking. Ask Stella. I even called you a hottie."

Sophie narrowed her eyes, suddenly feeling a lot more sober.

"That's to say—shoot! That didn't come out right either. I'm . . . you're . . . " The guy shook his head and looked completely dejected. "I'm sorry," he repeated. "I should've stayed at my table and just looked like an ass from a distance."

"Yeah, that probably would've been a good choice." Phew. Her voice came out polished and smooth.

The man winced. "I was toasting myself. It's kind of weird, I know, but there you go."

Curiosity niggled at Sophie, despite herself. "That is weird."

The man shrugged and looked down at his feet.

"Especially because I literally just toasted myself a few minutes ago, too."

It took a second for her words to sink in, but when they did, surprise and interest warmed the stranger's amber eyes to cognac. "Really? And what was your toast?"

Sophie cringed, then thought, why the hell not? She might as well get used to sharing her intentions. "It was about an upcoming New Year's resolution, actually—to stay single."

"That's not just weird. It's crazy." The man started laughing and Sophie was mildly offended, but it was short-lived. "That's what I was toasting—to Bachelorhood for the New Year and beyond."

Sophie wondered if that was an intentional play on the famous Buzz Lightyear quote, but decided not to ask.

They studied each other a moment, letting their mutual plans sink in, then lifted their glasses. "Well, here's to us then," Sophie said.

"And the single life," the man agreed. Unfortunately he didn't stop talking there, while he was ahead. "Anyway, you glanced over when I raised my cup. I could tell you thought I was coming onto you. I wanted to reassure you I wasn't."

Holy crap. Make it stop. It was one thing to say you were choosing to stay single. It was quite another to have someone rub your nose in how unattractive they found you.

"Well, thanks," she said drily, and for some reason, probably the mulled wine, she added, "I'm not attractive to you. I get it, and I'm fine with it."

He looked her up and down again, and her cheeks heated under his scrutiny. What the hell was his problem? He inhaled, appeared to gather his thoughts, and actually managed to be less of a goof when he spoke next. And damn it, this time his words actually fit the nice timber of his voice and gave her a shiver. "That's not what I said. You definitely *are* attractive to me—explaining, I guess, my flustered jackass routine. I don't speak to a lot of women, let alone hit on them."

"Because you want to say single."

He nodded. "Exactly. I just wanted to be clear I wasn't making some move, in case I made you uncomfortable."

Well, mission unaccomplished. She was definitely uncomfortable. Thankfully, Stella appeared with a huge plate piled high with roasted carrots and turnip, baby potatoes, slabs of meat, and a glorious Yorkshire pudding.

She put the food down in front of Sophie, but instead of telling her to enjoy her meal, she pinned the visiting man with a glare. "Jesse Ales, you'd better not be harassing this woman." Stella's gaze, still stern, shifted to Sophie. "Is everything okay here?"

"Yes, Stella, of course. God," said the man named Jesse Ales.

"Er—"

"If he's bothering you, Sophie, I'll tell him to get lost."

"Well, he's not *totally* bothering me. He was just letting me know I don't need to worry. He isn't hitting on me."

The expression that shot across Stella's face at Sophie's words—and the look of disgust she threw the man—made Sophie giggle.

"Jesse," Stella said. "Back to your own table. Now."

Was she his sister or something or just well used to him being a weirdo in her bar? Either way, Jesse looked abashed. "Yeah, that's probably for the best." His downcast eyes found Sophie's dinner plate. "Uh . . . and maybe I will eat. Wanna get me a plate of what she's having? Please?"

He turned away, shoulders down, reminding Sophie of Pete, her bullmastiff, whenever she scolded him. "Sorry," he mumbled again. Then, "Ah, shit."

She glanced over to see what had caused this new ire. Someone was pulling his deserted table toward their own, making room for more people to join them. There were plenty of other tables and chairs. Heck, even with the small dinner rush, the place was still more empty than full. And yet . . . The words were out of her mouth before she could stop them, and Sophie rolled her eyes at herself. What was she doing?

"Wait, if you want, well, you can eat at my table since yours got nabbed."

"Are you sure? I mean, it won't be weird?"

Sophie shook her head. "It'll be totally weird, but that's okay."

A grin creased Jesse's face, and his mournful eyes brightened a little. Dammit. What was wrong with her? Why was she always a sucker for a guy with a problem?

As if reading her mind, his smile faded and he muttered, "Well, okay, thanks, I will. If you're sure you don't mind?"

She bit her lip and shook her head. "I invited you, didn't I?"

He was a little red. "It was a pity invite. Don't think I don't know it. Anyway, listen, I'm not always a loser like this."

"He's really not. He's usually a nice, safe, semi-sane guy." Stella scowled as she slapped down cutlery wrapped in a linen napkin and a dish of wonderful smelling gravy.

Sophie had almost forgotten she was still there. She laughed lightly and motioned for Jesse to sit. "It's fine. Relax."

She powered down her book, tucked it in the big bag beside her on the bench, and dug into her food.

"E-books, hey?" Jesse asked. "I've wondered about those. I'm a paperback guy myself."

"You're a reader?"

"Big time. Anything I can get my hands on—but fiction mostly."

"Oh yeah? Me, too." Sophie smiled as she considered him. He was built like whatever her imagination would conjure for a woodcutter or logger or something, but he was into books. Actually the beard did sort of give him a bit of a hot professor vibe. He really was kind of appealing—when he stopped being neurotic and weird.

She took her first bite and closed her eyes as a morsel of gravy-rich meat dissolved on her tongue. It was hard to describe the appreciation rolling through her—for her food, for her wine, for this evening so far from where anyone knew her at all, with this undeniably gorgeous man "not" hitting on her. She decided not to overthink it. To just enjoy the moment, whatever it was.

Chapter 4

WHEN HAD HE LAST HAD such a good time? Jesse shook his head and stretched. He and Sophie had talked the hours away, and though he'd matched her drink for drink and bite for bite, he was a little awed. Man, the woman could put it away. He loved it. And he loved how she enjoyed it so much, eating with abandon, with no excuses or apologies or pretending she didn't eat like that all the time.

She and Crystal were pretty much polar opposites appearance-wise—Crystal, as beautiful and fragile-looking as her name, all pretty angles and fair, fair skin and hair. Sophie. The soft, voluptuousness of her name fit her satiny dark hair and full curves perfectly. But it was the differences in their personalities—or what he'd learned of Sophie's so far—that really intrigued him.

She read almost ten novels a month, but thought his book a week habit wasn't too shabby. And when she asked what genres he liked best, his heart jumped a little with stupid pride when she nodded and grinned approvingly at his cheesy line, "Love one woman. Love many books."

She was a kindergarten teacher, loved it, and was a complete workaholic. (Said completely unapologetically.)

Didn't have children. Had never been married.

Wouldn't elaborate on either subject.

She drew cartoons.

"Oh, yeah?" he said oh-so-cleverly, but that was another nice thing about Sophie. She seemed to take their conversation for what it was worth. He didn't feel any pressure to be anything other than what he was—probably because he really couldn't be any less articulate or more awkward than he had been when he first introduced himself, and she'd still given him a chance.

"Prove it," he added.

Her eyes crinkled and she did. She drew a cartoon guy on the paper coaster. It looked just like him. The title made him laugh out loud: "Suave Jesse uses smooth lines and charm to make a new friend." She added a speech bubble: "I, er, uh, oh, hehmmm." He laughed harder. He got out of his chair and slid onto the bench seat beside her so he could see her work better. She smelled lightly of patchouli and citrus.

She turned toward him and cocked her head. He became aware of her warm thigh so close to his beneath the table. "What do you think?"

What did he think? Oh, man. He couldn't even begin to articulate it. He rested his fingers on hers. She didn't move her hand. "I think it's great," he whispered.

And yet he didn't realize he was in trouble. That didn't happen until she stole a coaster from the table beside them and created another character—a female she labeled "Sucker Sophie."

Oh, shit. He really liked this girl. And worse, he wanted her. Really wanted her. It was probably just the alcohol racing through him, spiking his heart rate, making him twitch and ache in places that hadn't twitched or ached or wanted in too long . . . but then again, maybe, just maybe, all the nagging busybodies in his life were right. Maybe he needed to get back on the horse, as his cousin Dave—idiot that he was— always said. Maybe he needed to take a shot one more time, just in case he could have happiness. *The horse.* It was a terrible analogy for a relationship. No woman would like it. Despite that truth, a chorus of terrible riding jokes jumped into his alcohol-compromised brain, and he thought they all sounded really good.

As his and Sophie's night progressed and their physical distance shrank while their conversation deepened, Stella had flitted back and forth to their table like a manic sparrow, with ever increasing agitation. Now she was announcing last call.

"I'll get you a cab, Jesse," Stella said, so pointedly that he wondered what her problem was. She was usually head of the You-Need-To-Try-Again Club.

He looked at Sophie. Sophie looked at him. Her pretty white teeth tugged at her plump bottom lip.

"No, I'm good," Jesse told Stella. "Thanks

23

though." His full attention danced to Sophie again. "Let me walk you to your hotel."

She gave him a scrutinizing look. "Walk me to my hotel or come up to my room?"

He grinned and shrugged. Then followed her lead because he liked how she just put things out there. No games. "Your room. Your bed. Your choice."

"I thought you were all into staying single."

"Hey, I'm proposing a hookup, not marriage."

For a second, the sparkle in her eye seemed to dim, but then her big smile returned and he figured he'd imagined it. Her answer made his heart pulse and his jeans grow tight. "Well, come on then, suave Jesse."

He and Sophie bundled up and left the warm bar together. Their breath mingled in little white puffs in the crisp dark air. Overhead, the night sky was a crush of navy velvet, full of brilliant stars and promise.

He kissed her before they even entered the hotel lobby. Her lips were cold, her nose frozen, and then suddenly, they weren't. He deepened the kiss, pressing her against the smooth stonework of Greenridge's oldest establishment and reveling in the softness of her body under the firmness of his. And he didn't know if he'd make it to her room. God, they hadn't even done anything yet and he felt like he'd come home. How the hell had he ever thought he'd be able to live without sex for the rest of his life? What was he, a total idiot?

Her mouth opened to him and her tongue flicked his. His whole body responded. Flick me, flick me.

"Wait." He unfastened the top buttons of her red wool coat—so perfect for a modern Snow White. Then he pressed his lips to her cool throat and kissed his way down her neck. She stretched against him, and he wanted to growl. He *did* growl. "We should go to your room. Now."

She broke free of him, laughing, and took his hand, pulling him out of the frigid darkness and into the glowing lobby. "Well, come on then."

Her fancy room was immaculate, suitcase closed, nothing out of place. She caught him looking around as she removed her jacket and slid out of her boots. "I'm here one night and one night only!" she announced like a circus ringleader, making him wonder if she was as nervous as he felt and trying to hide it. Then her voice softened. "Why bother unpacking, right?"

"Right," he whispered back and shucked off his outdoor clothing too, letting it fall where it lay, glad he'd had a shower earlier and hoping he wasn't wearing embarrassing underwear. Standing there, inches from her, both fully dressed but in their stocking feet already felt crazily intimate.

She smiled up at him, put her hands on his hips, and tilted her face toward his. He put his arms around her. It had been a long time since he'd been close to a woman, or even really wanted to be, but his inner animal remembered all the delicious sensations as his fingers played with the hemline of her soft sweater, lifted it, and rested on the silken skin of her lower

25

back. He traced along the waistband of her jeans, then dipped lower. He felt the unmistakable texture of lace trimmed satin, and his breath quickened. She shivered, still meeting his eyes, so open to him, so frank faced and willing. He wanted to kiss her again, but was suddenly unhappy. He already knew he didn't just want to kiss her for one night. This wasn't him.

She misread his hesitation, bit her lip, but kept eye contact. "I . . . don't do this all the time or anything, or well, ever, actually."

She leaned in a little and the gentle swell of her stomach pressed against him.

Stop thinking, he commanded himself. Do what men have been doing since the beginning of time and just enjoy it. She'd felt his erection and gyrated lightly, as if to feel it more. He obliged, gripping her hips almost roughly and thrusting toward her. Her eyelids lowered to half-mast and her cheeks were rosy, her lips swollen from their earlier kisses. The layers of clothing between them were torture.

"You're not attractive," he murmured. "You're a friggen sex pot."

"A *sex pot*?" Her giggle made his whole body hum. "What are you, eighty?" There was only teasing in her voice though, no veiled criticism.

He walked her backwards to the bed, lifting her arms over her head, freeing her from her sweater. Her bra was killer. Hot pink and black lace. The cups only half covered each breast and pushed them up like some

1950s pinup or something. "That's—wow," he said.

She smiled like he'd actually managed to say something coherent. And then they were on the bed, his shirt was off, she was stroking him, and they were kissing. And though, in practical terms, they'd hardly even gotten started, he already couldn't tell where she ended and he began.

"Tell me if I'm going too fast," he murmured at one point.

"Mm-hmm," she said and kissed his nipple, then took it into her mouth, nipping slightly. He thought he'd lose it right there, but somehow managed to hold on. The good news was that if he did blow his load too soon, he was sure he had another round in him.

He undid the button of her jeans, unzipped her fly, and saw a flash of that crazy pink satin again. Matching bra and panties. Dang, he liked that. So much.

She lifted her ass and shimmied out of her jeans. He could see her muscles moving under the luxurious softness of her flesh. She didn't seem to care one whit that the lights were on. It was the sexiest thing.

When she was free of her pants, he pulled her on top of him. She straddled him, satin panties against his straining denim. She traced a heart over his chest with one finger. He caught her hand and kissed it.

"Arch your back. Lean away from me," he said.

She raised an eyebrow.

"I want to look at you."

"Oh, yeah?"

"Yeah." He wanted to remember how she looked at this moment—warm and willing and wanting him—forever. Not that there was a chance in hell he'd forget. He felt like she'd branded him or something.

"And I want to feel you."

She tried to reply, but her words were lost in a deep sigh as he smoothed his hands down her ribs, cupped her waist, then clasped her ample butt. When he slipped his fingers lower, she was warm and ready and, oh, damn . . . He could stay like this forever. Suspend time. Never have it end or have to deal with any repercussions.

He played with her lightly. She moaned.

"Hey," he whispered.

Her eyes fluttered open with effort, like she was already set to go off herself and was holding back. "Hey," she echoed, her voice a butterfly wing of breath and sweetness.

"This is really nice," he continued. Understatement. Understatement. Understatement! "But I think I need to fuck you now." He didn't have time to rethink his classless words; a velvet rush against his busy hand told him she liked the words just fine.

She rolled off him onto her back, knees bent. He positioned himself between her legs. Her bra was still on. Her panties too. He smiled down at her, willing her to know how grateful he was for this . . . even though he suspected the morning would be hell for him. And he was just deliberating the smoothest way to remove his jeans and simultaneously make her pantie free, when he saw a shadow flicker in her eyes, something that conflicted with the sensual happiness in her expression.

"What is it?" he whispered.

She shook her head and stretched to kiss his shoulder.

"No, seriously. What?"

She sat up beneath him. He leaned back on his haunches.

"I'm not that drunk."

"All the better to remember me with?"

She chuckled, but looked sad. "That's the problem."

He didn't know what she meant by that. What problem? He studied her body language, noticed that she'd crossed her arms over her chest. Oh no. No, no, no. "I don't think . . . This isn't a good idea. It's not me."

Dammit. Disappointment replaced arousal so quickly it almost made him dizzy, and suddenly he wasn't buzzed anymore either. "Are you sure?"

She cringed. Covered her face with her hands. "Yes. And I'm so sorry," she repeated. "I was—I *am*—so attracted to you. I wanted to try this out, see if it could work for me. It's not. I just—"

"No explanation needed." Her sweater had landed across the room, so he passed her his shirt.

"Oh, don't be so nice about it," she moaned. "I'm

29

really sorry."

He shook his head, sighed. "I can't lie. I'm sorry too." He pointed at his dick, still making a proud showing. "And so's he."

She looked up at that, saw where he was pointing, and cracked half a smile. "Aw, Suave Jesse's sad too?"

He laughed in spite of every frustrated part of himself. "Oh, no, you didn't? Suave Jesse. He was my dick the whole time?"

She shrugged and grinned—then looked thoroughly miserable once more.

"Hey." He chucked her gently under the chin, making her meet his eyes again. "Don't worry about it. I'm serious. Suave Jesse, er, I mean, *I* will survive. Honestly, one cold shower or a sock and some lube and we'll be good." What? Had he really said that? Man. Kill him now.

But she smiled again, almost looked like she might laugh, so maybe sounding like a complete tool was worth it.

He got off the bed, pulled his jacket on over his bare chest, and turned back to her. She was still wrapped in his shirt and had pulled the hotel bed's throw blanket over her legs.

"Is it because you're scared?" he asked. What was he expecting? Her to be as crazy as him and say something that matched the insane thoughts running through his head, something to the effect of, *I just feel like I like you too much even though we've just met and it's nuts, but I don't want to mess things up by acting totally casual when I feel anything but.* Right. Like she'd say—or was feeling—anything remotely like that.

Her brow furrowed. "Maybe," she said matter-of-factly. "Yes."

He nodded. "I'm not asking anything of you or expecting anything. You don't have to worry."

Sophie's head tilted to the side and her expression closed a little. "Thanks."

So that was that. The end of their night. "Okay, well, it was nice meeting you. You're a great person, and I had a really nice time. Thank you." Lame. Lame. Lame. He wanted to add, "Have a good life, okay?" but it would sound sarcastic and he meant it sincerely. He settled with, "Safe travels tomorrow, okay?" and hightailed it the hell out of there.

Chapter 5

December 27th

SOPHIE INCHED ALONG THE FRESHLY plowed drive into River's Sigh B & B, trying to take in every sight at once. She was so gobsmacked by the scenery that for a few minutes she forgot the nightmare-person she'd been the night before. The sun was a silvery ball of light, looking every bit like the massive star it was, sparkling and twinkling in the pale white-blue sky. It glinted off the thick crystalline frost that coated all the leafless trees and lit the snowcapped mountains and white-robed evergreens with a beauty that almost hurt.

And then she was rolling into the main parking area and pulling her little black rental car to a stop in front of a shingled house with a bright blue door. The home's multi-paned windows glowed with warm light, and its wraparound deck was decorated with garlands of real pine, white lights, and tiny cranberry red Christmas balls.

A tiny wood plaque hanging from a quaint wrought iron frame said "Office," and she smiled at the pretty planter of cedar boughs, ribbons, and holly beneath it. If her cabin was half as nice as the grounds were so far, she was going to have a lovely time—and would fully recover from her humiliating mistake. What on earth had she been thinking? She couldn't care less what other people did, but she wasn't a one-night stand kind of woman. In fact, she wasn't an *any-kind-of-stand* woman anymore. No, the only reason she hadn't vetoed the rest of the holiday and tried to get an earlier flight home was that Jo had promised her River's Sigh was remote. To her huge relief, it was. There was no way she'd accidentally run into Jesse here.

Jesse. Dammit. How had he gotten under her skin in such a short time? How long would it take for the memory of his cedar and spice scent and the sexy roughness of his hands on her skin to fade? Well, it didn't matter. It would take as long as it would take— and here, in the complete privacy and incredibly romantic setting of the very isolated River's Sigh B & B, it should go faster. Thankfully, Jesse thought she was leaving town. Even if he was interested in seeing her again—and really, why would he be, she was a pub night fling that hadn't panned out—he wouldn't know she was around to find. She ignored the stupid pang in her chest that thought set off.

"Sheesh, you're pathetic," she muttered as she knocked on the office door. "Just thank your lucky stars you don't have to look him in the face and confront your humiliation ever again."

Not a sound came from inside, so she knocked louder, then pulled her loose wool hat lower over her ears and tugged her scarf up. Yes, it was beautiful here—but holy cow it was cold too. She should've worn her red coat, not just a heavy sweater. Still no answer. She turned to survey the yard. Maybe the caretaker, no doubt some white-haired Mr. or Mrs. Santa type—if they were as magical as the rest of this place anyway—was doing outside chores.

Sure enough, just across the way, a human form emerged from around the corner of a cute-as-a-button cabin marked "Minnow" with a funky fish-shaped sign. The figure straightened when he saw her and picked up the pace. There was something familiar about the man's stride. And did she recognize the gray felt parka? Wait a minute—

No.

No.

No.

She glanced this way and that, looking for an escape route.

The man raised his hand. "Hey, there. Hello! Sorry, I wasn't in the office. I wasn't expecting you 'til later. You're Rita S. Printz, I take it."

The voice, even at fifty yards, muffled by a scarf, confirmed it. He hadn't recognized her yet, but man, oh, man—

Sophie didn't realize she'd been stepping back and back and back on the porch until she smacked, hard, into the shingled wall.

"I'll grab your key, show you around."

Jesse was up the stairs in a leap, but before his feet even settled on the porch's wooden planks, startled recognition jumped across his features. He tore off his scarf, as if removing it would help him see more clearly or make her disappear.

His voice was hoarse. "What are you doing here? You said you were only in town for a night. And River's Sigh isn't officially open. I'm just helping out a friend. There's only one booking. For an elderly woman. A—"

Sophie shrugged, hating that she already recognized his babbling as a nervous tell. It wasn't like they really knew each other. She shouldn't feel like she had any inside knowledge of his inner workings. "For Rita Sophia Printz. That's me. My legal name. I go by Sophie. I'm not particularly elderly though."

"Oh." He was still looking at her with an expression of near horror that probably mirrored her own. "No, uh, no, of course not."

She shook her head. "Okay, um, this is awkward. It's all right. I'll just head home. I don't mind paying for the cabin or whatever for a night or two as a kill fee."

Giving Jesse a wide berth, she started down the stairs.

"Wait."

She didn't want to do any such thing, but then

again, it wasn't like he'd engineered any of this. It was just an . . . unbelievably embarrassing turn of events. Was this why some people cursed small towns? You couldn't avoid your mistakes at all. She'd barely been in Greenridge twenty-four hours and she'd already made a huge mess.

"You can leave, of course." He looked like that was exactly what he wanted her to do. "It's just, well, I'm supposed to be helping Jo and Callum out. I really don't want to have to explain why their paying guest left."

That struck Sophie as hilarious—and kind of sweet. Apparently it didn't even occur to Jesse that he could just lie, or omit the particulars.

"It won't be weird," he promised.

"Uh huh," she said skeptically. Hadn't one of them said something similar the night before? Yes. And hadn't it gotten weird for her? Yes. Potential-damage-to-her-stupid-heart-again weird. Already. After just one long dinner and a close booty call? What was wrong with her?

But her return flight wasn't booked for another eight days. She could change it, but even that would take time. She sighed and then disregarded the warning alarms pulsing through her stomach. "Okay . . . as long as it won't be weird."

Jesse raked a hand through his hair. "Right then. Good. *Good.*"

It didn't take a genius to hear how insincere his

words were. He didn't feel it was good at all. He was just as disturbed by the turn of events as she was—yet another thing they had in common, drat it anyway. He's a womanizing, pub-crawling, one night fancy man, she reminded herself. She smacked her forehead with her palm. *A one-night fancy man*? What was she, some early nineteenth century spinster?

Concern bordering on consternation flashed across Jesse's face at the slapping sound. "Well, okay then. Let me grab your key and show you around."

Chapter 6

HIS DAMN HEART THUDDED SO hard the whole time he led Sophie about that she probably heard it. Why did she have to be so nice, commenting on every little "cool" thing Jo and Callum had done to the property and being utterly thrilled by the cabin? He wished she was a snooty, hard-to-please bag or something.

"It's like a fairyland. . . ." Her voice trailed off as he pointed to the forested path that wrapped through the various cabins and meandered all the way to the creek. Jo and Callum kept the path clear for walkers, and Jesse had freshened it up, in case she wanted to explore. Before Christmas, Jo, Aisha and Sam had strung rope upon rope of tiny white lights through the trees and shrubbery that lined the path, and well, yeah, he guessed it was pretty.

He tried really hard, and failed just as hard, not to compare Sophie to Crystal. Crystal was the kind of woman who actually prided herself on being high maintenance; Sophie seemed to like everything she saw without reservation.

He knew he was quiet to the point of being rude as

they trudged through the crunching snow, giving only one or two word descriptions and directives—path, creek, other cabins, your cabin—but he couldn't help it. He was completely unsettled by her.

Finally she was ready to move into her home away from home. He helped her bring her suitcases into Rainbow cabin—two cases, not just the small one she'd had at the hotel. No, strike that thought. He was not going to think of them at the hotel ever again. And then he helped her bring in groceries and a box of bottles of wine. Yes, a box.

He figured all the food was a good thing at least—an actual good thing, not just a polite good thing like he'd expressed to Sophie when she said she'd stay. When Jo told him he only needed to prepare breakfasts, he'd wondered if she was being optimistic, if the guest would know how remote River's Sigh was and how far it was from any restaurants. Apparently he could lay that fear to rest. Sophie looked well capable of taking care of herself. All he'd have to obsess over was being on his best behavior at breakfast, controlling himself at any outings they went on (One of Jo and Callum's brilliant requests, that he offer to take her sightseeing, curse them!), and not being weird. Right. No problem there. Shit.

This would all seem more manageable if he wasn't totally sleep deprived—and if the cause of his sleep deprivation wasn't walking beside him, smelling so great, smiling so widely as she took in every detail of

River's Sigh, and generally being a huge thorn in his side. He hardly even knew Sophie. Why was he so obsessed with her?

And on that note, as politely as he could, he let her know he was staying in the main house if she needed anything, asked what time she'd like breakfast the next day, and fled.

As he headed back to the office, a huge cedar bough above him chose that moment to unleash a cascade of snow from its heavily burdened branches. An icy spray dusted his head and fell in chunks down the back of his jacket, and he had an epiphany.

He didn't know Sophie. Right. That was the whole answer to his problem. He could relax. Throughout the next few days, thrown together by chance as they were, he'd get to know her better. And once he did, as had happened every rare time those old, cruel desires for a relationship stirred in the years since Crystal disemboweled him, this fledgling attraction, infatuation, or whatever, would fade, and he'd return to the safety of his happy-to-be-single status.

Chapter 7

WHY HAD SHE KEPT HIS shirt? Sophie unfolded and refolded the soft, well-worn flannel long-sleeve. Walked it into the kitchen and set it on the counter. Picked it up again. Shook it out, then bunched it close to her face and burrowed in her nose in it. Why did he have to smell like that? She'd never been particularly aware of Kyle's scent. She'd spent a few hours with Jesse and wanted to eat his up.

She'd kept the shirt too long. Giving it back now would be super awkward. She should've returned it the second he entered the cabin and dropped off her suitcases. Now he'd think she'd held onto it on purpose. Or maybe he wouldn't even remember. Maybe he went home shirtless after . . . events that she preferred not to think about . . . too many times to count. Maybe his tongue-tied shy act and his graciousness when declined was all just a pantie dropper technique. Or maybe it wasn't. Either way—why did she even care? Whatever. She retreated, shirt in hand, back to the master bedroom and shoved her contraband into the nightstand's open-faced shelf.

She sat on the bed, bouncing lightly. River's Sigh B & B had fancier cabins, but Rainbow was her imagination's picture-perfect wilderness getaway—with enough luxuries to make it extra fun. She sighed with happiness, but had to admit, drat it anyway, she felt more than a tinge of longing, too. It would be such a lovely place to retreat with someone special. She sighed again, more heavily. So this was it? Her destiny: to say and act like she was happily single, had chosen to be, in fact, all the while, deep down, pining away for the fantasy: wuv, twoo wuv—and mawage.

She really, truly had thought Kyle had killed all that in her. Or maybe she'd just hoped.

Wow, way to wreck a lovely moment, Printz, she nagged herself. Buck up. Put food on, get an art envelope done, and then you can go outside and play. That did make her smile. A real smile.

"Only you would bring your own crockpot on a vacation," she mumbled aloud, teasing herself but actually loving that quirk in her personality. She gathered and chopped, filling the hefty pot with diced onions, minced garlic, sliced carrots, dried peas and other goodies. Then she poured in vegetable stock. Even though it hadn't remotely started to cook yet, it already smelled good. And when she came in from outside later, it would smell more than good. It would smell heavenly.

Dinner set to be ready in six hours or so, suitcases unpacked, soothing hot Chai for company, Sophie sat down at the small dining table and got to work on her New Year's art envelope. She liked to create cross-curricular activities to reinforce every lesson she taught and to appeal to the widest variety of learners and skillsets. The range of developmental maturity for fine and gross motor skills, emotional and mental school readiness, etc., was all over the map for five-year-olds (maybe for every-year-olds!), so for each early concept she introduced, she found or invented some sort of art project, a way to incorporate movement or action, plus a related story to help plant the seeds. Some people didn't understand working with five-year-olds or consider it "teaching" per se. Even her own sister called it "glorified babysitting." And it was true, even after all her years at it, Sophie continued to be surprised by how often little kids cried—and had accidents in their pants. That said, she really believed what she was doing was valuable. Her kids might not remember what she taught them specifically, but she prayed she made them excited and confident and eager to tackle new things—and that such an attitude would stay with them for life.

She'd been a December baby, so a bit younger than the bulk of her classmates every year, and a dreamer personality. Until college practically, she was always a little less sophisticated and mature than everyone else—or so she thought. Later, she realized she just wasn't as good at faking it. She couldn't feign disinterest and be "cool." She was spazzy, silly, and interested in everything. She had hated school initially and struggled—was made to feel stupid when things didn't come as quickly to her as they did to others. It was her personal mission that no five-year-old would ever leave her class in June, already feeling like academics weren't for them.

Her construction paper work done for one day, at least—who knew you could actually develop calluses from using scissors over time!—she put her things away. Then she found the two snowman building kits she'd assembled when she decided to take this trip and put on her specially purchased honest-to-goodness snowsuit. Catching the reflection of her puffy purple self in the window, she literally laughed out loud. She looked like an oversized nine-year-old and felt like one too. Yay for recess in the snow!

As she waddled into the big white space that was her cabin's yard, she smiled up at the sky. Fresh snow was falling, so thick and white that although it was midday, it seemed like there was no sunlight at all. The world around her was the soft, soft gray of a dove's underbelly and the quiet was as deep and full as a feather bed. Contentment filled her. Of course, she was planning to wreck the peacefulness with her car stereo and hip-hop music, but for now . . . ahhhh.

She didn't realize she was unconsciously looking for Jesse until she'd scanned the yard for a solid minute. He wasn't anywhere to be seen, though. He was probably bundled up inside—or maybe he'd gone to town. Jo had been clear that she'd be on her own most of the time and wanted to make sure that was all right. And it was more than all right. Of course. And really, what would she do if she did see him? Ask if she could steal his scarf to go with his shirt or something?

She decided against the car stereo after all, enjoying the deep calm, and set to rolling her first big snowball.

She thought again of her reticence to even entertain the idea of dating. She'd enjoyed herself with Jesse, totally, so why was she being so lame?

A moment with a student came back to her—a little firecracker named Candace Green, or *usually* a little firecracker, that is. The class went on a field trip to the swimming pool, and Sophie was shocked when Candace wouldn't jump into the water for anything, no matter which parent volunteer offered to catch her.

"I don't like to jump in water," she'd kept repeating resolutely. "I got hurt on a stump. I don't jump."

Sophie never got fully to the bottom of the stump story, something about a lake and a camping trip gone awry, but Candace had been unmovable.

Why was she thinking of that story now? And was that what she was doing, letting fear rule her? Maybe, but oh well. She could see little Candace's point. Yes, water was fun, and in some ways, she was missing out—but she also wasn't going to get smashed on some unseen hazard lurking beneath a pretty surface.

45

The snowball was huge; it was hard work to roll it to the final spot she wanted it to sit—where she'd be able to see it from the window—and she actually grunted with effort. It made her grin. Then she happily started the snowman's belly. She ignored the tiny questions that formed like shining icicles in the back of her imagination. What if Jesse wasn't a player, the kind of guy to almost make love to someone, then in the next breath say he didn't have any expectations, didn't want anything from her? What if he really was sensitive and kind, just strong enough to hold back his desire? What if he loved homemade soup? Or was the kind of grown-up who still played in the snow?

Yeah, and what if my snowmen came to life? Thumpety thump, thump, thump! She hefted the middle ball onto its base and started rolling a big round head.

Chapter 8

JESSE PULLED BACK INTO RIVER'S Sigh just as the sun was going down, and he decided to take a walk before he rustled up something to eat, wanting to clear his head.

The crew he'd hired to tear down a wall to create an open concept living/dining room and paint the interior of his house needed a weird amount of hand-holding. Maybe he shouldn't have told them he couldn't care less what colors they chose. As soon as he finally volunteered to go into the hardware store and pick out shades, they'd been much more normal. They figured they'd easily be done by the end of his stint at River's Sigh.

The timing was also excellent considering his new headspace regarding Crystal. He'd thought his desire to renovate was just the property owner inside him, wanting to keep the house updated so it held its value. Now the idea of neutral walls to showcase the art he'd started collecting thrilled him, as did the prospect of freedom from Crystal's oppressively trendy decorating style. He'd been unconsciously keeping the house like a memorial to her, but now he was ready to let go and move on from the hold she'd had on his home and his life.

And I arrived at that decision before I met Sophie. The thought was immediately followed by another: *Why the hell is that relevant?*

Jesse's feet hit a slippery spot in the snow and threatened to fly out from under him. He looked down. His truck's tracks were freezing and slick in the dropping temperature of approaching evening. He grinned, took a small run, and hopped onto the track, sliding a little—then almost losing his balance. He held his arms out, caught his footing, then ran and slid once more. Snow skimming! Maybe he'd invented a new sport. He did it a couple more times, then shaking his head at himself, jogged toward the forest path. There was something about winter he loved. Maybe just that it kept the hyper brat in him alive and kicking.

It had snowed heavily all afternoon and his cleared path was no more. Instead it bore a marshmallow layer of fresh deep snow. Ah, well, he'd snow blow again in the morning. There was no point expending the energy now when it was probably going to snow all night. No doubt Sophie was shut in from the weather and wouldn't be using it.

He flipped a switch on the outside of the maintenance shed. White lights glowed into being along the twist and turns of the path, muted by the heavy snow.

Only one small light shone into the deepening

shadows from Rainbow cabin. He wondered idly what Sophie was up to, hoping she wouldn't see him through her window and think he was stalking her.

Then he saw something that pushed his heart into his mouth. Made his blood pound. Two people stood, hiding at the edge of the forest, staring into Sophie's living room window.

"You there, hey." He charged off the path, through the deep snow, into Rainbow's yard. "Hey!"

A woman shrieked, obviously terrified at being caught up to no good. And how was he so sure she was up to no good? Why else the shriek?

"What is it? What?" The female voice still sounded extremely startled, but he recognized it now. *Sophie.* What the hell? Jesse stopped in his tracks and looked around. Then he grew impossibly warm, despite the chilled air. He had valiantly rushed in to save her from . . . snowmen. Or, more accurately, snow persons, a Mr. and Ms.

They were both decked out in splendor worthy of a made-for-TV Christmas movie: A top hat, featuring a blue band decorated with holly, and a blue and green checked scarf for him. A raspberry red knit hat and shawl for her. What looked like genuine coal for their eyes and mouths. What definitely were real carrots as long, perfect snow people noses.

Sophie jumped up from where she was crouched and moved to his side, staring in the same direction he was, but definitely searching for something more

49

ominous than what held his attention. "What is it?" she repeated. "Is there something in the bushes?"

He wanted to say, yeah, a wolf or a bear, but he wasn't really a liar. Just terminally stupid. He shook his head. "No," he said glumly. "I was just trying to protect you from the onslaught of lurking snow people."

Sophie's brow furrowed. She glanced from Jesse to the snow folk then back to Jesse again. And then her cheeks dimpled with a huge grin. "Oh! You mean you thought they were real? That actual people were creeping around my cabin?"

He shrugged and wished he could fall off the face of the planet. "Yeah, uh, well, it's almost dark and I was distracted. I saw their shadowy figures and—"

"*Their shadowy figures*?" Sophie burst into what could only be described as peals of laughter.

Ms. Snowman's lumpy smile seemed on the verge of a giggle too, and Jesse realized he was being dumb all right—but in the reverse of how he'd first thought. Why was he embarrassed? It *was* funny. Hilarious actually.

"Well, one can never be too careful, right?" he said. "But have no fear. Under my watchful eye, *snow* harm will befall you."

Sophie fluttered a red mitten over her heart. "My hero! I'm *snow* relieved you were here to save me."

They stood grinning at each other and their corny word play. Jesse didn't know what was cuter: Sophie's groan at his "snow harm" line, how she snort-laughed at her own joke, or how her nose and cheeks were bright pink from the cold. He looked at the snow people again and took in her outfit. She was wearing an actual snowsuit. "You must've been out here for hours," he said.

She shrugged and her cheeks went even rosier. "Yeah. There's never a lot of snow in the lower mainland. I've been looking forward to playing outside ever since I booked my flight." She motioned toward the well-dressed snow couple. "It's kind of silly, but I made kits for their getups from stuff I ordered online. I bought an igloo brick maker, too."

"A what?"

Yep, she was definitely blushing.

"A plastic thingamajig you pack with snow to make uniform bricks so you can build a fort."

"Oh, yeah, I've seen those. What else?"

"What do you mean, what else? Isn't that enough?"

"No, so fess up. If you were Internet binging for some dream play fest, you had to get something else," he teased.

Her shoulders hunched in silent laughter and her face creased in merriment. "Okay, okay, you're onto me. I did get one other thing."

"What? You did? I was only kidding."

"One should never kid about toys or games. They're very serious things."

"I'm starting to see that, yes."

51

"It's called a snow art kit. It comes with idea sheets, plastic molds, and super fun colored sprays—environmentally safe, don't worry."

"Oh, yes, I was worried, but now? Phew." Jesse raised his hands in mock relief.

She laughed and without discussing it, they both turned and tromped back toward Rainbow cabin's door. "I was about to head inside, just before you, ah—"

"Totally rescued you."

"Yeah, that's it. *Rescued* me."

He raised a hand in a casual farewell when they reached her small porch. "See you for breakfast tomorrow."

"Yep, no earlier than six-thirty a.m., no later than nine, right?"

"Well, I don't know. In light of the scare you had this evening, and considering I'll be puttering around here all day tomorrow, I can probably be flexible if you need me to be." He liked the lines that crinkled by her eyes when she tried to suppress a smile. Really liked them.

"So I'll surprise you then."

"Sounds good." It did. It definitely did.

It was all of three steps up the porch to the door, but he waited to see her hand safely turn the knob before he walked away. Behind him, the door opened and the hearty, fragrant aroma of cooking food wafted out, steamy and good in the night air. The door clicked shut. He smiled, picturing her playing in the snow,

now clambering into her kitchen, pulling off her snow pants and eating soup and crackers for dinner.

He was halfway back to the main house when her voice stopped him.

"Jesse, wait." He turned to see her beckoning from the porch. "Have you eaten yet?"

"Uh, no . . . " He took a hesitant step toward her.

"Well, do you want to? Eat with me, I mean. It's just soup—"

"I'd love to."

She was backlit by the light pouring from the doorway, but even with her face mostly in shadow, he knew she grinned. He could feel it.

"I'd totally love to!" he repeated, then ran back the way he'd just come—and purposely slid, skimming the snow the best he could.

"Whoo-hoo, look at you," she called. "Show off."

They played Scrabble after they ate—the best soup he'd ever had for the record—because, in her words, she wanted to prove she could do more than color and build snowmen (like he had any doubt). She kicked his ass, then taught him a speed game, using Scrabble tiles, called "Take Two."

She grumbled and complained when he beat her three times back to back. "Beginner's Luck."

"Skill, pure skill," he countered.

They both thought they were hilarious.

And while they didn't touch physically once the whole evening, Jesse left her cabin just after midnight feeling like she was wrapped around him, closer than close. He liked it.

And it terrified him.

Chapter 9

December 28

SOPHIE REMOVED THE TRAYS OF purple, pink, red, and blue colored pasta, all assorted shapes and sizes, from the oven. The food-colored water she'd dyed them in before baking them at a low heat had done a fantastic job. When they were cool, she'd stick them into resealable plastic bags, and tomorrow she'd do another batch, maybe yellow, orange, and green. It was always funny to her how much the kids loved the pasta play station. They counted and sorted the pasta, cleared space on the bottom of the high-sided table and created long repeating patterns, made pasta necklaces, and begged to use vehicles from the You Can Drive It station with it. Pasta was second in popularity only to the water table and bean bin. Kids were kind of like cats in that respect, the simpler and less expensive the toys, the more fun they had. They'd clamor with great excitement over some expensive toy-of-the-minute pushed by the media, but at the end of day, what they used the most were playthings where their imaginations were free to roam, unhampered by the preset rules and plots that came with licensed toys. Or the lucky kids did anyway. Yep, get a cat a box. Find a kid a stick. That's all they needed.

Prep chore done for the day, she glanced at the clock. Eight-thirty. It felt like the ultimate in luxury to not already be in her classroom, waiting to entertain, comfort, and challenge young minds—to be, instead, on her way to a breakfast cooked by her very own personal chef. She grinned. She had to remember to call Jesse that when she saw him. She knew he'd like it.

What are you doing? an inner voice nattered.

"Enjoying my holiday," she said aloud. "Immensely." And she was. Sometime during the Scrabble game she'd realized he really wasn't going to make their first night's encounter weird. There was nothing wrong with forming friendships. Was she never going to have a friend of the opposite sex again just because of Kyle? No. Being friends with Jesse was probably the best way to push the idea of him as a romantic interest from her mind. After all, most of a romance centered on the fantasy elements you bestowed on the object of your interest without them even knowing it. Getting to know him thoroughly would reveal who he actually was: a nice guy who wasn't for her.

Uh huh, the nattering part intoned again. She ignored her slightly sarcastic inner voice, pulled on her jacket and boots, and happily trekked across the unblemished field of white.

Her peaceful contentedness was sadly short-lived.

They were eating at a small bright yellow table in the kitchen because the formal dining hall was way too big for two people. She had insisted it was fine for Jesse to eat with her, that she'd prefer it actually. He made waffles with real whipping cream and strawberries for breakfast, and they had hot chocolate powder in their coffee. "A lazy man's Mocha," he called it.

"Lazy's perfect for a day like today." She inhaled deeply, then was hit by a huge yawn.

"Did you sleep all right?"

"Wonderfully," she assured him. "I'm just in vacation mode, happily sluggish."

They made chitchat while their food disappeared, then Jesse asked, "So what made you take a holiday for one?"

That simple question was where it all went wrong, so terribly wrong.

"Well, it's kind of related to the toast I told you about the night we met. It's this new lifestyle thing, sort of an experiment, where I aim to not only accept, but to strive for and embrace perpetual singlehood."

"What does that mean?"

"Well, for one, not only do I not pursue romantic relationships, I actively try to avoid them."

Jesse laughed—a bit bitterly, she thought. It should've been her first clue that her explanation was falling on deaf ears. Some things you should keep

57

close to your chest because they were too off the common beat to chat about with just anybody. But in light of recent events, she failed to remember that "just anybody" might still include Jesse.

"Yeah, about that. I did say 'try to avoid.' I'm sorry about the other night. I wanted sex, but figured I'd regret it in the morning."

Jesse made a disbelieving, derisive snorting sound. She frowned. Even if she was getting her wish and seeing the side of him that would squash her crush, it didn't feel good. "No, the other night was fine. What I'm not swallowing is your claim that you want to stay single."

"No?"

"No." He shook his head and pushed back from the table, then refilled her coffee without even asking if she wanted more first. "There's no woman alive who doesn't want the ring, the dress, the white picket fence, and the whole shooting match."

Sophie barely managed to refrain from spitting out her coffee—but refrain she did. She forced herself to swallow and dabbed her mouth with a napkin. "No woman alive, hey? Wow."

Jesse shrugged. "I'm just saying, deep down, no matter how much any woman says she values her independence, yada, yada, yada, it's a ruse. She wants a husband-slash-provider, and if a new, better version of what she has comes around, she'll trade up the second she can. It's biology."

"So . . . you're not only saying no woman alive would ever willingly be single, you're saying every woman alive is also a shallow, unfaithful gold digger?"

"Well, not quite. I just mean, well, I call bullshit is all."

"You call bullshit is all," Sophie parroted back slowly. Then, before he could say anything else, she stood up and looked around. "Wait, did you hear that?"

Jesse followed her gaze, looking uneasy all of a sudden.

"It's the phone. 1954's calling and it wants its dick back."

Jesse's brow furrowed and he rubbed his beard—which no longer looked at all cute. He looked like he should be starring on some stupid reality TV show, featuring backwoods assholes. He opened his mouth to say something else, but she cut him off. "Oh, sorry. My mistake. Wrong number. The '50s are over—and guess what? Women wanted independence from male chauvinists then too."

"I'm just saying that in my experience, women—"

"And I'm just saying, regardless of your experience, women are, *gasp*, individuals. Some want similar things and some want totally unique things and some want a mixture of things and some don't know what they want."

"And you're saying you want something different?"

"Dude—I'm not saying what *I* want to you, period,

because it's none of your damn business!" *Dude*. Why did that word have to be her go-to when angry? It was ridiculous sounding—yet she'd made her point, she thought.

She strode to the door, overriding her innate desire to help clear and tidy the kitchen. "Thank you for breakfast, but don't worry about feeding me for the rest of the week. I'll fend for myself."

She shoved her arms into her coat sleeves and didn't bother to do up the buttons. She turned back to Jesse for a second. "And I also have to say three more things. One, I don't know why you're suddenly being so mean and rude, but I don't like it. Two, I'm sorry I resorted to sarcasm. It's a bad habit when my feelings are hurt. Three—which is also sort of a four and five. I thought we were becoming friends, and I'm sad that isn't true. I'm glad you tipped your hand about the kind of person you are, though."

Jesse's mouth fell open, but if he said anything in response, she didn't hear it. She opened the door, shut it firmly, and stepped out onto the porch. A cruel wind kicked up and made her regret her impulsiveness. She took the time she needed and securely fastened all of her buttons, all the way up.

Back in Rainbow cabin, she called her sister Kate. She had promised she would once she was settled in and was long overdue—but she also wanted to vent.

"Why didn't you call me right away when you got in?" Kate said in lieu of hello.

"It's a long story," Sophie admitted.

Kate cut in after the bulk of the tale was told. "Well, he's kind of right. About you, at least."

"What's that supposed to mean?"

"Well, you actually do want to be married. You just have a very specific guy in mind. This whole modern-nun thing you're playing at is just a front."

"What the hell? You actually buy his line of misogynist crap?" Sophie rushed the aluminum teakettle over to the sink and filled it with water, more to vent some of the energy bolting through her than out of any desire for tea. "Well, news flash. Not all women do want to be married. Or to be financially or emotionally or any-other-way-in-the-world dependent on a man."

"I don't disagree with you a bit—with two exceptions. Marriage doesn't have to equal financial or emotional dependence. If it's healthy, it's a true partnership, regardless of who brings more money into the house. And I'm not talking about *women;* I'm talking about *you.* And you do want to be married—or at least to have someone to love and share your endless energy and appetite for fun and life with. So in that way, Jesse was right. What you said was bullshit. You and I both know, whether you'll admit it or not, Kyle burned you good and you're scared shitless. Besides, this Jesse guy might not have been saying exactly what you thought he was saying anyway."

Leave it to Kate to play devil's advocate and take a male stranger's side over hers. "Whatever," she said as flatly as she could.

There was a second's pause, then Kate added, "Of course, there's also the very real possibility that you're right and he's a complete idiot. Either way, try not to let him wreck your holiday. It sounds marvelous. I can't even imagine a whole week of solitude."

The last line held a hint of longing, and Sophie's irritation faded. Kate loved her big, rowdy family—but it was no secret that sometimes she wished she and Sophie could change lives just for a few weeks.

"Don't worry. He won't wreck anything. I won't let him."

Kate sounded a lot like Sophie's inner skeptic. "Uh huh."

Chapter 10

JESSE HAD TOLD SOPHIE HE'D be staying on the property all day—but that was before the breakfast debacle. Now he was cruising along the highway as fast as the slippery road safely allowed. What had gotten into him? Why had he acted like such a total ass? It was one thing for him to be lost for words or awkward. It was something else entirely for him to be a jerk and take his shit out on an innocent person. And not only had he come off as some woman-hating oaf, he'd completely insulted the paying guest he was supposed to be catering to. Jo would have his hide. And if Jo didn't, Callum would.

Jesse could only imagine what Sophie's guest feedback card would say. Then again, whatever the stupid card said was the least of his concerns. He'd hurt her feelings. She'd taken what he'd said personally. And why wouldn't she? He'd directed his comments at her—and totally out of the blue, when she was only answering a question he'd asked.

His brain replayed the last bit of their interaction over and over again. Sophie striding to the door.

Shoving her coat on. Then, despite her outrage, taking the time to explain why she was hurt and angry before she left. If the tables were turned, he would've stormed off and been done.

He found himself back at the hotel pub. It wasn't open yet, but Stella let him in anyway. "You can eat breakfast with me."

"I already ate, but I'll nurse a beer, if you don't mind."

"It's ten-thirty in the morning! I know you're a regular, but God help you if you end up like some of the regulars."

"Fine. I'll have a coffee. With beer in it."

She brought him a coffee.

"Thanks, Stel." A few sips in, he set his mug down and sighed heavily.

Stella looked up from her hash browns with something like alarm. "What's wrong now? I thought you'd be over the moon after your conquest the other night."

He scrubbed a hand over his face. Right. She'd seen him leave with Sophie. Awesome. "It wasn't like that. It's not what you think . . . or not quite."

Stella leaned in, her expression suddenly brighter. The brightness faded as he relayed the events of the past few days, however. "Well, obviously you're just projecting your issues about Crystal onto Sophie."

Weirdly, he didn't want to talk about Crystal. She felt like an old scar now, not a current wound. It pissed him off that she might still be in his head, messing with his life against his conscious will.

"It doesn't matter *why* I did it. It matters *that* I did it. I hurt Sophie, and she's, well, pretty great."

Stella put her fork down and stared. "You really like this girl? You weren't just wasted?"

"Come on, Stella. In real life, stone cold sober or fall-on-my-ass drunk, have you ever known me to attempt a one-night stand? I wouldn't have even left the bar with her if I didn't like her."

"But then you guys didn't, um—"

"No. She changed her mind. That was a bit uncomfortable in every way you can imagine, but it was also a good thing. I was getting cold feet, too."

"Why? Actually, no, forget I asked." Stella stood and started clearing away her half eaten food. "Jesse, you're one of my oldest friends. . . ."

Oh oh. That didn't sound good. "Uh huh?"

"I think you should take this whole Sophie thing as a good sign. I've never seen you like this after any of the disastrous dates you've been on since Crystal left, not even the ones that led to more than one date."

"Okay . . . " He still had no idea where she was going with all this.

"Look, Sophie's from out of town, so you knew nothing could come of it. That was probably a big part of the attraction, actually. But then you started feeling close to her, so just in case there was a chance something might develop, you unleashed that stupid tirade to protect yourself and create an obstacle that would effectively end things."

"I thought you said it was a good sign."

"It is. I'm getting to it. She's not from here, so nothing can really grow between you, but you want it to. *That's* the good part. It means you're finally ready to move on. To have another relationship. A real one. There's someone out there for you, closer than you know. You just had to open your eyes—and now that's happening."

Jesse got up and helped himself to more coffee from the pot behind the bar. When he sank back into his seat, he muttered, "Yeah, yeah. You're probably right. I think you're right."

Stella leaned back in her chair, arms crossed, and studied him. "Don't sound so depressed. Like I said, even if it feels bad right now, it's a good thing. It really is."

Right. A good thing.

She got up and unlocked the front door. Two boys, barely legal age from the look of it, staggered in. "Oh, no, out you go. You guys have already had enough." They complied with only a bit of fuss. A group of five entered.

"Do you serve breakfast?" one of the women asked.

"You bet," Stella said.

Jesse continued to sip coffee and think while Stella bustled about and fed people. She was right about what caused his outburst with Sophie. Dead right. It didn't excuse his behavior, but at least it helped him make sense of it.

He had started to care for Sophie. But was that good? It sure didn't feel like it. Especially since, as Stella repeatedly pointed out, Sophie was temporary. She had a life elsewhere. She was leaving. And in just five days or so.

He ingested still more coffee. Finally, an hour or so later, feeling slightly queasy, he headed back to River's Sigh. He knew what he had to do.

His plan was hijacked minutes away from the River's Sigh B & B turn off. Flashing red and blue lights stopped him.

Two cop cars flanked either side of the highway, and an ambulance was just leaving. No siren though. Was that a good thing or a very bad thing? A mess of skid marks cut through the crusty berm on the road's shoulder. Impossibly far off the road, almost to the tree line, the snow was badly disturbed. A red pickup sat nose down, butt up, buried to its box. Jesse turned his focus to the police cars again—then caught a detail in his peripheral vision that churned his guts and turned them to water. A small black car, whole passenger side caved in, squatted on the opposite side of the road. The torn up circles of gravel and salt on the highway suggested it had whipped around in pirouettes before it careened off. It took him a second to understand the dread in his stomach and to put all the pieces together.

Oh, shit.

Oh, God.

No. *Sophie*.

67

Chapter 11

SOPHIE STEPPED FROM THE HEATED patrol car into the slapping cold. Yikes, it was brisk. She was glad she'd packed her snow pants, a candle, and a blanket into the rental car, even if she had rolled her eyes at herself when she'd done so. What if the accident hadn't been reported so quickly? Or what if she'd gone off the road alone in the middle of the night or something? She would have needed them. She buttoned her coat higher and tucked her hands under her armpits.

"Okay, well, we have your contact information, Ms. Printz, but it should be pretty straight forward with the insurance company." Constable Julette nodded in the direction of the pickup's driver. "He claims full responsibility. If you have any problems with the adjuster, just have them call me."

As much of a headache as an insurance claim involving a rental car would be, Sophie figured she should be grateful. She couldn't have had a better witness than an RCMP doing highway patrol. She thanked the officer again, started around the side of the police car—then froze. She had no way home, duh.

Her car was totaled and the tow truck would take it wherever the rental company directed. They were handling all that now, and they'd bring her another car later.

"Excuse me," the other officer, not Julette, appeared at her side. "Do you know this gentleman? He insists he knows you, says he can give you a ride home."

A tall bearded guy approached from the rear of the squad car, as if cued. Jesse. Of course. That was her luck in a nutshell, wasn't it? She hadn't noticed him drive up or seen him standing there, talking to the police. Maybe she was more rattled by the accident than she'd thought.

"Yeah, I know him," she mumbled.

The officer's demeanor instantly changed, and she treated Jesse like he was Sophie's next of kin. "We suggested she go to the hospital, just to be sure she didn't hit her head or get whiplash or something, but she insists she's fine. And a first aid attendant seemed to think she was too."

"Because I am, thank you."

A tow truck rolled up, the driver confirmed who she was and which vehicle was hers, and things wrapped up fairly quickly from there.

All there was now was the trip back to River's Sigh, alone with Jesse, to be stranded in the remotest bed-and-breakfast known to man—okay, that was a slight exaggeration, but still—also with Jesse, completely reliant on him for transportation until the details for a substitute car were ironed out. Delightful. Just effing delightful.

Chapter 12

SOPHIE, SEAT-BELTED INTO HIS TRUCK, arms wound tightly around herself, leaned as close to the door—and as far from him—as possible. She could have been one of those pictures counselors use to help people identify emotions in others. Jesse wasn't always good at reading cues—understatement!—but this one was loud and clear: I am still angry.

"Are you okay? Are you sure you weren't hurt?"

She sighed. "I'm fine. Just a bit shook up."

"Yeah, no kidding. Looks like you spun in circles."

"Yeah. The guy T-boned me." She stared out the window.

"Are you still angry with me?"

That got a look. "Yes."

He nodded. "And you're uncomfortable being with me now."

Her eyes narrowed. "Uh, yes, again. Are you hoping for points or something? You can read me. Bully for you." She paused. "Sorry, all sarcasm aside. Yes, I'm still pretty irritated—and yes, I feel awkward being with you."

Jesse's studded winter tires chewed up the miles between them and their destination. He swallowed hard and pushed on while he had a chance. Sophie was almost uncomfortably forthright about how she felt. When he'd asked if she was still angry, he'd have bet money that she'd just shrug or avoid eye contact or something. Stop assuming she—or any women—are all like Crystal, he commanded himself. *Trust her.* He didn't deserve it, but maybe if he tried to emulate her, strove to be as truthful, she'd give him another chance.

"I'll understand if you don't forgive me, but I want to apologize. I put a bunch of stuff on you that I didn't even know I was holding on to. It wasn't fair. I was reacting out of anger toward my ex and transferring it to you. Probably because I was scared by how close I felt to you after such a short time. I think I was trying to put up a wall or something."

Sophie shifted in her seat to face him, and one of her eyebrows lifted. "Wow, that's a pretty abrupt change of tune, and a pretty well-articulated bit of self analysis. What did you do, go on a four hour Dr. Phil binge when you left River's Sigh?" Her tone, thankfully, was softer than her sharp words suggested.

Jesse put on his signal light and slowed the vehicle. They'd be on River's Sigh B & B's long driveway in seconds and then, after a few minutes that would pass too quickly, he might lose her, even as a friend. He had to be careful. He had to say his next words just right— though he suspected it wasn't the phrasing she'd care about. It was the honesty behind whatever he said.

"I didn't figure it out by myself. Not even close. I talked to my friend Stella. You know her. You guys met at the bar the other night. She served us."

Sophie's eyes widened. "You talked to her about . . . us?"

About us. The words sounded bizarre. But also right. Thank God he managed to keep that to himself, however. He didn't want to scare her off forever. "Yeah." He nodded. "I felt terrible about the things I said and how I offended you. I really like you too, and feel honored getting to know you. Also—and this is crucial—I don't believe the shit I was spouting. I really don't."

Sophie gave him an appraising look, but her eyes were a little warmer. "And if I asked Stella if this was out of character for you, or if you actually are a completely misogynistic weirdo, she'd say . . . ?"

"She'd say I'm definitely a weirdo and that I've been a self-pitying, slightly bitter jerk since my divorce, but it's a hate-people-in-general thing, not a hate-women one. Not at all."

"Just people *in general*?"

"Right!" he exclaimed, relieved she understood.

She shook her head, but laughed. "I guess that's better . . . maybe."

The main house came into sight. Shoot! Any second, she'd pile out of the truck, go to her cabin, and maybe never give him the time of day again.

He pulled to a stop in the same place he'd parked earlier in the day, cut the engine, and turned sideways in his seat. "Look, I truly meant what I said. I've loved getting to know you, but it was the last thing I expected, so it's scaring the shit out of me. The only thing that possibly scares me more is the idea you might write me off right now, that we might never . . . see where this takes us."

"Shit," Sophie said. "Shit, shit, shit."

It wasn't quite the response he was hoping for. (Understatement, yet again!)

She pressed her bare hands to the slightly foggy passenger window then held her palms to her red cheeks. "Apology accepted." Her voice was very soft. "And I feel the same way, dammit."

"Why dammit?" he asked, totally digging this ask her a direct question, get a straight answer thing. She was a very refreshing person.

She sighed and held her hands to her face once more. "Well, as I told you . . . I recently decided to embrace single life. Being interested in you, even remotely, even though I'm only here for a week, isn't going to help me with that resolution. And if I end up really liking you, I'll be hurt when it doesn't work out. And if I end up not liking you, that sucks and might make me even more leery of relationships than I already am, and—"

Jesse held up his hand. "Let's cross those bridges when we come to them, okay? We don't have to plan how we're going to mess each other up when we haven't even—"

He'd been about to say "haven't even kissed yet," but they had, of course. And then some. Suddenly his whole body was suffused with memories of them, and he was tongue-tied. "When we haven't even, uh . . ."

Sophie leaned over and pressed her lips chastely to his cheek—then not as chastely to his mouth. His whole body surged. "When we haven't even what?" she asked a second later, eyes glinting. "Officially gone on a date?"

"Exactly."

"Well, I'm free . . . right now. We can go for a walk to the creek because even though it's silly, I'm kind of nervous going into the forest by myself."

"It's not silly at all."

She smiled. "And then you can wine and dine me. And after that, you can give me a backrub. The ambulance guy warned I might be sore later."

"I have an idea," he said.

"What?"

"How about you tell me exactly what you want to do and then we'll do that."

She wrinkled her nose, smirking a little. "Am I being too bossy?"

He shook his head, then nodded, and grinned at his own joke. "Yep, and I love it. One question though."

"Oh, yeah?"

"Yeah. What's on the agenda after dinner?"

She turned pink. "I guess we'll just have to see, won't we?"

Jesse went around the side of his pickup to open her door, warring emotions bouncing through him like crazy. He wanted to jump around and give imaginary friends fist bumps and high fives because she was giving him a second chance and seemed to return his feelings. He also wanted, desperately, to just escort her to her cabin and say so long because he'd been here before. He'd gone all out, no holds barred, and no matter how badly he was falling for it, there was no way she was what she seemed to be. No one could be so genuine and up front about things, not for real.

Chapter 13

SOPHIE COULDN'T BELIEVE HOW FAST the day passed or how full it had been. Was it really just this morning that she and Jesse fought, that she'd been in an accident? She inhaled deeply, taking in their surroundings, and marveled at how quickly all of life changed.

Jesse had brushed off a huge limbless log and stamped down the snow around it, creating a picturesque outdoor couch. They sat snuggled together, sipping hot chocolate that he'd brought in a big thermos, and watched the creek below them. They listened to the odd bird, spotted a rabbit, and sometimes just sat, lost in their own thoughts—but mostly they talked. And talked and talked. Of light things like hobbies and favorite foods, but mostly of deeper things, like their childhoods, what they wanted out of life, and their careers.

Jesse was, of all the things she never would've guessed, a landlord. He'd purchased properties, his first at just nineteen, when the area was in a recession. Now he owned a variety of single and multiple family dwellings, in addition to a small twenty-four-unit apartment building.

It should've seemed forced or contrived to talk this much, about such serious things, when they'd known each other for such a short time, but that was the thing—biggest cliché in the world—it felt like she'd known Jesse forever. Or that she should have.

The only topics they steered clear of were the stories behind why they'd both found themselves alone the day after Christmas, making solitary toasts to a New Year's resolution to stay single. She knew he'd been married and divorced and had "baggage" because of their earlier conversation, but he shied away from giving any details.

And conversely, when he asked about the "serious" relationships in her past and whether she'd ever been married, she'd fought to keep her voice light. "Ah, you know, a close call here or there, but nothing that stuck."

The words were true, but how she passed them off as casual and no big deal felt like the worst kind of lie. After that, she shifted the conversation to easier subjects—more book talk, more food chat, and silly holiday memories from their childhoods.

"What about pets? Do you like dogs?" he asked at one point, almost urgently.

"Love them. I have an ancient bullmastiff named Pete. He's at my sister's while I'm away."

Jesse nodded with something like relief, and Sophie looked at him curiously. "You?"

"I had a good ol' girl named Molly—a border collie shepherd cross."

He sounded so sad that Sophie took his hand and squeezed it. "What happened? Did Crystal get to keep her after—"

"Crystal? No, she hates dogs. It was a bone of contention between us, actually." He tried to grin, but it didn't reach his eyes, and Sophie couldn't muster a smile for his pun or let him lighten the mood just yet. "So what happened?"

"She just got really old and passed away, about six months ago."

Sophie squeezed his hand again. "I'm sorry. That's really sad."

"Yeah. Thanks."

They sat without talking for a while, and the shelter of the snow-draped evergreens kept the worst of the wind away and blocked all sound. Sophie didn't think she'd ever heard such deep layers of quiet.

Every so often, though, she caught a whisper from the nearly frozen creek and understood the bed-and-breakfast's romantic name. Iced up and snowed over in most spots, the creek would've been almost invisible except for the enormous snowy rocks that jutted here and there, suggesting a creek or river bed. Yet every so often a spot burbled and frothed—or sighed—showing that life still teemed beneath the seemingly dead surface.

Eventually, even through her heavy snow clothes,

Sophie got chilled, but she didn't want to leave this place, this moment.

"How are you doing?" Jesse asked, putting his arm around her and tucking her close. "Frozen to a lump yet?"

They'd been quiet for long minutes, and it was both companionable and frightening. Sophie knew full well this sweetness between them was just part of her vacation. There was no way she and Jesse could develop anything of lasting value in a mere week, but she wanted to enjoy it. Savor it. She really did. However, lame as it was, she was already feeling sad about saying goodbye. Not that she was about to admit it.

Earlier, Jesse had said something about her "complete honesty" in an admiring tone. If only he knew. She was a naturally straightforward person, true—but she'd also learned there was value in appearing unguarded, and she sometimes used her disarming statement of facts and willingness to tackle uncomfortable topics as a deflection tool. If you say something hurts you, it loses its power to whomever you've said it to, and no one suspects how deep the hurt actually is. And if you confess you're afraid, people automatically think, "Wow, she's brave. She admitted that she's scared." No one sees your true, bone-deep terror.

"What are you thinking about?" Jesse asked.

She lifted her chin and let herself get lost in his gaze. Then she motioned around herself. "Just that this . . . you, me, here together right now, meeting like we did, having all this to ourselves . . . It's pretty perfect, isn't it? A fantasy come true."

Jesse pulled off a rough wool glove and traced the curve of her cheekbone. "It doesn't have to be a fantasy. It could be real. We could make it work. We should definitely at least try to."

"Yeah," she said, smiling. "Definitely."

A shadow darkened his eyes, and he studied her a moment before lumbering to his feet and extending his hand to help her up. "Wining and dining awaits you, as commanded."

"Oh, goodie." She bounced to her feet, no help from him necessary, and dusted off the seat of her snow pants with her mittened hands. "What?" she asked, a tad disconcerted by how intently he was staring at her again.

"I know you're not buying into this whole you-me potential relationship as wholeheartedly as I am," he said. He reached down and tipped her face to look at his. "And that's okay. I'm totally fine to just see where we end up—but a quick heads up, I intend to do my best to win you."

Somehow the slightly old-fashioned sentiment managed not to be corny coming as it did in his low, growling purr. A tremor that had nothing to do with the cold walked down her spine. She opened her mouth, though to say what exactly she wasn't quite sure.

He pressed his finger to her lips. "Think up something funny or clever to say later. Right now—" He pressed his mouth to hers; he was cold and tasted of chocolate. And before she could register surprise or pleasure at the impromptu kiss, he was deepening it, opening her mouth with his tongue, tasting her, teasing her, making her want . . . more.

It was the first time they'd kissed since Pub Night, as she'd taken to referring to that first evening they'd almost hooked up, and she had to admit a big part of her had wondered if she'd imagined or exaggerated the flaming attraction that burned between them. This simple outside kiss blew that notion away, kindling a yearning that weakened her knees and left her hollow in the center with want. It had never been like this between her and Kyle. Never.

Jesse broke the kiss, and Sophie sagged against him unsteadily. Damn, she was so transparent. He smiled, and she saw a gleam of smug pride in his face. He knew how much he'd gotten to her with one— albeit long and sensual—lip lock.

He ran his hands up and down her arms, as if to warm her. "I should feed you before you starve."

Usually she'd insert a smart aleck comment there, something like, "Do I look starving to you?" etc., etc., but her wit had deserted her, replaced by a humming awareness. She did feel starved. For Jesse. How could you want someone, need someone, so strongly when you'd just met them? It didn't make sense. None at all—and she knew it all promised one thing: an inevi- table heartbreak that would make Kyle's humiliating at-the-altar dumping feel like a walk in the park.

She realized Jesse was waiting for a response. "Dinner, right. Sounds great."

He looked at her for a long time, then nodded and took her hand. As he led her out of the forest, she tried to ignore how good their entwined fingers felt, how right.

Damn, she was going to get hurt again. So hurt.

Somehow though, in the soft quiet that yawned between them as they walked back from the creek, she managed to rally and cheerlead herself into not being such an idiot. Don't wreck anything before it needs to be wrecked, she lectured herself, and it worked.

They had a lovely, if surprising "first date" dinner—fish and chips with a green salad. Somehow, the simple, completely unpretentious meal was just the right thing.

"I do cook," Jesse assured her. "But this is fast and easy and leaves more time for . . . anything else we might get up to."

"Oh, yeah? And what's this 'anything' you speak of? Dishes? Snow plowing?" she teased lightly, though the heat in his eyes made her whole body tingle.

After quickly cleaning up the kitchen, Jesse inclined his chin toward the unseen rooms beyond. "Want a tour?"

She shook her head, a bit surprised at herself. Normally she'd love a tour of a place like this.

"We could take over the living room. Jo and Callum won't mind—"

She shook her head again.

He looked at her. "Okay, your turn to think of something."

"It's pitch black outside now, not just dark."

"Uh huh?"

"So you could walk me over to the center of the parking lot. We could pretend we just slipped through the wardrobe into Narnia, and you could kiss me under the falling snow in the golden glow of the streetlight."

She expected him to laugh at her, and it wouldn't have bothered her if he did. She was being pretty goofy, after all. He didn't though. Instead, he reached out and traced her mouth with his finger. His eyes were soft and serious. "Under the falling snow in the golden glow, hey?"

She shrugged. Why was she so dumb sometimes?

He moved suddenly, throwing open the door. Powdery snow swirled in on a breeze. "Well, come on then."

"What?"

He grabbed her hand. "Run. Run!"

She did as bidden—tearing into the snowy yard after him, both shoeless and only wearing socks. "What about our coats? Our boots?"

Jesse laughed and only tugged her more insistently. And then they were standing beneath the bed-and-breakfast's solitary lamppost. Beneath its light, which did indeed look golden against the dark sky, the snowflakes were illuminated magic. Until now, Sophie had only related the feeling that your heart might burst with joy to the pages of stories, not real life. Now she knew differently, and she felt it might change her forever. You could be with someone who made your heart feel full to bursting.

"I couldn't wait for us to put on coats or shoes," Jesse whispered, tilting her chin up toward his. "I couldn't wait one more minute."

They kissed, and when Sophie finally opened her eyes, about to step back, Jesse stopped her, firming his hold around her, keeping her close. "Meeting you, being with you, totally feels like I really have fallen into Narnia or some other magical place," he whispered. "And I don't want to go back, ever again."

Sophie agreed, oh how she agreed. But she knew about magical places; they never seemed to work out for mere humans. Yet she didn't say that. She just sighed—deeply, happily—at the moment, at him, at *them*, and kissed him once more. She wasn't going to utter any words that might break the enchantment.

Slowly, slowly, Jesse walked Sophie backwards to her cabin—a delicious stumbling walk, where he kept his body pressed up against hers and basically kissed her along, step by step, until they were at Rainbow cabin's porch. Sophie didn't know about Jesse, but her feet were so past cold that they were numb. The fuzzy socks she was wearing had collected so much snow it looked like she sported boots after all.

"Do you want to come in?" she asked shyly.

"I do," Jesse said in a solemn voice, making her giggle.

Before they opened the door, by silent and mutual agreement, they tugged and pulled off their snow-bogged socks. Then they eyed their pants, snow encrusted to the knees. Jesse grinned and shrugged, then shucked off his jeans. Sophie shook her head, but copied him, tugging off her leggings one leg at a time—it was bizarrely difficult to remove wet leggings—until she stood shivering in her tunic-styled shirt.

Inside Rainbow, Sophie wasted no time. She ran a lukewarm tub and called for Jesse. They sat on the edge of the tub and inserted their bright pink feet and calves.

"Oh," Sophie squeaked. "Ouch."

"Yeah, scalding, right?" Jesse agreed.

They didn't talk, just smiled at each other from time to time and made swirls and waves with their feet.

When her feet, still not warm, but at least not blocks of ice, started to prune, Sophie drained the tub. Then she reached for a towel and one of Jesse's feet. At first he resisted, but she smacked his calf lightly. "Hold still."

He laughed and obeyed, letting her rub him down.

And then he dried her feet. The soft cotton towel felt oddly rough and, even more oddly, somehow sensual as he patted down her calves and ankles and scrubbed her arches. She giggled and pulled away when he touched her big toe. "No toes. No toes!"

"Is someone ticklish?" he asked, but mercifully didn't go on to torture her.

They still had matching bright pink extremities as they padded to the living room. "Wait here," she said and disappeared into the bedroom.

"Penguins or unicorns?" she asked when she returned.

He shook his head at the two pairs of fuzzy sleep pants she waved his way. "How am I supposed to take myself seriously and manage to seduce you wearing those?"

She grinned. "Okay, unicorns it is."

He caught the ball of purple and pink fabric she tossed. "And why's that?"

"You know. They're horny."

"Ahhhh, that was terrible. You're killing me," he moaned.

"I'm hilarious and you know it."

His eyes crinkled again.

They both pulled on the pajama bottoms; the unicorns bagged at Jesse's butt and came to a flapping end just beneath his knees. She started laughing. "Okay, you're right. Those are not hot on you."

"Thanks a lot."

There was heartbeat's pause.

"Wow," Jesse said, finally.

"Yeah," she agreed. "This, that is to say, *us* . . . it's

87

a bit crazy, hey?"

Jesse sank onto the couch and pulled her onto his lap. "So you feel it too?" he asked. "I mean, I'm not trying to jump the gun or scare the shit out of you, but it's kind of intense. Like we've been together forever in all the best ways, but also—"

"Like everything about how we've met and how we are together is rare and new and..." Sophie trailed off.

"Yeah, like that. Totally," Jesse said.

One of his hands made its way under the back of her shirt, and he stroked her lower back in soft, deep circles. It felt incredibly good—but brought the stiffness between her shoulder blades suddenly to mind.

"Hey," she said. "That reminds me. You were going to rub my shoulders."

"I can think of other things I'd like to rub more."

"I bet you can," she said with arched primness in her voice. "I'll just bet you can."

She moved off his lap and onto the carpeted floor. He spread his legs and she nestled between his knees, then sighed as he began to knead her neck. "Mmm, that feels good."

"I'm glad," he said.

She reached for the remote. "Want to watch a show?"

"Sure."

She selected a Christmassy romantic comedy.

"Oh, my favorite."

"Seriously?"

"Nope. Not even remotely."

She laughed and went to select something else. He stilled her hand. "But for now it's great. It's perfect. I won't be paying attention anyway."

She shrugged and settled back once more. "Suit yourself."

He leaned in and kissed her jaw from behind, then her neck. "Thanks, I will."

She wondered if he felt her shiver.

Maybe he did—but did he misinterpret it as a chill, or rightly intuit her response to even his simplest touches? Either way the results were the same. "Scoot forward," he said.

She did and he slid off the couch, straddling her from behind so that she was cozily held in the V of his body, his arms snug around her.

The night danced on with teasing butterfly-light touches and some heavier moments, too, but they didn't go further than kissing and cuddling—and she knew she'd never forget the movie that serenaded them. From here on out, it was destined to be her holiday favorite, even if she'd never tell another living soul about why.

He didn't act disappointed that nothing more happened. The idea of more didn't even come up. They just seemed in tune, relishing the slow get-to-know-you moments, enjoying the ache of desire and the promise that waiting to satisfy it would make it all the more gratifying when and if they did.

The final scene ended, the credits rolled, and eventually Jesse sighed and pulled away from her. She was immediately colder.

"I should go," he said. "It's late and the sooner we sleep, the sooner we can enjoy tomorrow."

Part of her wanted to stop him, tell him to stay. A bigger part of her knew herself. She was in too deep already. Sex with Jesse would never be casual for her and no matter how much she longed for it in some ways, separating was going to be hard enough as it was.

Still, she couldn't actually bring herself to say the words that would force him to leave.

He smiled down at her, then got to his feet and pulled her to hers. "I feel the same way," he said. He pressed a kiss to her forehead, gave the hand he still held a squeeze, then released her.

She stood at the kitchen window and watched his trek through the blowing snow, laughing softly at his horny unicorn pants fluttering in the breeze around his knees. Just before a stand of three huge cedars that would steal him from view, as if he felt her eyes, he turned and raised his arm.

She waved back, her heart simultaneously heavy and full. She'd really set herself up for a fall this time. And she couldn't, at this moment anyway, bring herself to regret it.

Chapter 14

December 30

JESSE WOKE, OPENED HIS EYES, and blinked. Sunlight glinted diamond-bright off the frosted bedroom window and threw small rainbow triangles onto the wall. He hadn't turned the heat up last night, and the air on his face was cool while under the blankets he was toasty. It was a delicious contrast. He could get used to River's Sigh B & B. Staying in Jo and Callum's guest bedroom felt like a proper holiday—or maybe it was the company he was keeping. Either way, he stretched lazily and stayed put a moment, enjoying the warmth and softness of both the comfortable bed and his recent memories. How on earth could he have only known Rita Sophia Printz for four days? It felt like four years—and like four minutes. *Sophie.* Her name was like music in his brain. Yet she would leave? She'd go? That didn't seem possible either.

Those thoughts got him out of bed fast. It was already the thirtieth. She was leaving on the fourth. They had no time to waste, and he'd figured out how they should spend the day. He couldn't wait to see her face when he asked her.

"Tobogganing?" she said after a pause. Her face was soft and lightly creased with sleep, like she'd just crawled out of bed. Maybe she'd been sleeping in when he knocked. Suggesting she go back to bed—with company—was suddenly way more appealing than the idea of careening down ice-ridden hills at a hundred miles an hour, but it was too late. She shook her head, and the action instantly dislodged her sleepiness. "That sounds fantastic!"

So tobogganing it was. He stopped by his sister Maggie's house and borrowed her kids' snow toys, leaving Sophie in the truck with the engine running. His niece and nephews clamored to go with him, and were only slightly mollified when he promised to take them on their own again soon.

"You actually have a flesh and blood woman in your pickup and she's going sledding with you?" Maggie didn't even try to be subtle. She leaned out the door and craned her head, trying to see into his passenger seat. The windshield had fogged over, however, thwarting her attempt to spy.

"Yes, she's real, thank you very much. It's kind of awkward to bring a blow-up girlfriend to a tobogganing party. They pop when they get too cold."

He thought the blow-up part was the line she'd focus on. But as ever, he didn't have a clue.

Maggie's eyebrows shot up so high they disappeared into her thick bangs. "Wait a minute, your *girlfriend*? She's not just a living, breathing female, you actually think of her as your girlfriend?"

Jesse shook his head. Why had he thought this was a good idea? He should've stopped at one of the big box stores, spent a hundred bucks, and spared himself the third degree. "I don't know why you think it's headline news that I'm with a woman, and no, she's not my girlfriend. That was a joke about—ah, never mind. Forget it."

"I don't think it's news. I think it's a friggen miracle!"

"Thanks for making this so easy, Maggie."

Maggie laughed. "No problem, little brother. No problem."

Trudging back to the truck, dragging the sleds behind him, Jesse realized this too was a sign he was better. Maggie hadn't given him any wide-eyed looks of concern. She'd just harassed him. Other people must think he was healing up okay, too.

They got fast food for breakfast and ate in the truck as they headed to a gravel pit Jesse knew had views and sledding that were second to none.

Down they went again and again, laughing and shrieking, the spray of fresh snow dusting their hair and faces and coating their clothes like powdered sugar.

Finally, coming to a tumultuous stop at the end of how many runs Jesse had no idea, Sophie stood up on the black plastic sled they'd determined flew the fastest, then plopped onto her butt again. Her cheeks were flushed, and her eyes sparkled under her wool hat.

"Phew." She shook her head, and her words formed white plumes in the cold air. "I want to go again, but I can't climb that hill one more time. I just can't."

Jesse lay back in the snow and stared up at the endless sky. "Thank goodness," he said. "I actually thought I might die on the last two climbs—but thankfully, I still have enough energy to make a snow angel." He waved his arms and legs back and forth, pushing the snow beneath him into an angelic shape to prove it.

"Yeah, not being able to make an angel to celebrate the day? That would be a tragedy." Sophie threw out her arms and copied his actions. When her own angel rested behind her, Jesse reached for her mitten-clad hand and they lay there together, breathing deeply, looking up. Above them, billowing clouds waltzed across a pearl gray dance floor. Jesse never wanted it to end. Never.

Chapter 15

EVERY MUSCLE IN SOPHIE'S BODY was numb with exertion, but in a good way—a hole up for the afternoon with a book and hot chocolate way, so that's what she did. She'd spent so much time with Jesse the past seventy-two hours that her heart felt like it had been tobogganing, too. It was fluttery and overheated with excitement and thrill, but suddenly a bit overwhelmed by it all. She needed a break to recoup and think.

When they got back to River's Sigh, Jesse seemed to understand her need for alone time and cheerily left her to her own devices for a while.

"We have all the time we need," he said. "Four more days here. Then we'll make plans about how to see each other in the future."

His words made her stomach flip—in a happy way or a terrified way, she wasn't quite sure—but then he was saying something else, and she forced herself back to the moment. "I had a really good time," he said. "I've never gone sledding with just another adult before."

Sophie laughed. "Me neither."

"So, uh, would you like to go out for dinner tonight, or would that be too much of a good thing?"

"Not at all. Dinner sounds wonderful. Is seven too late?"

They made their plans and Sophie settled into the cabin for the afternoon. She read. She drank cocoa. She even took a nap. But snug in a cozy nest of blankets on the couch, she also thought about everything that had happened the past few days, and she wanted to pinch herself. What she was feeling couldn't be real. Jesse couldn't be real. She liked everything about him. His silly sense of humor that matched her own so well. His soft, gentle nature wrapped in a rugged, gruffly handsome exterior. The way he seemed so sure they'd go on to be something more than they were now. And what about that? Was that what she wanted too? She didn't know if she was brave enough to risk things not working out in order to see if they *could* work out. But sitting in this perfect place, anticipating yet another evening with this seemingly perfect-for-her man, she wanted to be.

AT FIRST THE RESTAURANT SEEMED lovely—plus, it was fun to dress up and show Jesse she wore something other than fleece and snow pants occasionally. Before they'd even ordered, however, Sophie began to wish they'd stayed at River's Sigh for dinner, either in the main hall with Jesse cooking or in Rainbow cabin with her cooking.

Being out in public felt . . . different. Their magic bubble was more like a fishbowl. Unlike when she went out with friends back at home and they could easily choose a restaurant where they wouldn't see a soul they knew, everyone in the place knew Jesse—and wanted to stop and talk. And she was definitely under the community's microscope, but she wasn't sure why. Was there something specific they were trying to gain by sizing her up, or was it just nosiness? And also, was it just her, or was it strange that people kept accosting Jesse with small talk when clearly they were on an intimate date, complete with fancy clothes, flowers, and candlelight?

Jesse, as much as she kept telling herself she was imagining it, was ill at ease, too. He kept one elbow propped on the table and shielded his face with his hand as they talked. If you could even call their idle chitchat *talking*. Was he shy about being seen with her or trying (ineffectually, she might add) to stave off more visitors?

His face, which she was so used to seeing wide open to her, was strained with unhappy tension.

"Are you having a good time?" he asked about a zillion times.

There was a limit, however, to how often she could paste on a toothy smile and say, "Oh, yeah. Wonderful." The night went from borderline terrible to flat out awful from there.

By the time they finished their first drinks and appetizers, Sophie had been introduced to no less than seven friendly Greenridgers. She excused herself to go to the ladies' room, which was located at the end of a long hallway, conveniently near their table, but hidden discreetly from view by a large ornamental screen.

Sophie took her time. She didn't really need the toilet, just some respite. Finally, realizing she'd accidentally been gone long enough to be considered rude—or cause worry that she'd run into a problem—she headed back along the hallway. As she neared the screen providing her and Jesse's table's privacy, she heard her name spoken by a female voice and froze.

"I know you think you like Sophie," the voice was saying. "And I get it, I really do. She seems like a great gal."

Gal? thought Sophie.

"But be realistic. She's not from here. She definitely has city vibes—or general weirdo vibes. She's not like us."

The speaker's voice was familiar, though Sophie couldn't place it immediately. Whoever she was, she said "city vibes" like they were worse than "general weirdo vibes"—whatever that meant. But that wasn't the comment that shoved a screwdriver into Sophie's chest and turned it. It was the "She's not like us." That was always the case for her, wasn't it? Even when she finally relaxed and felt like this was it, she'd finally found a niche with people, or a specific person, someone always realized what she'd known all along. She was different somehow—and not different in that offbeat, intentionally funky way some people were. Different in a way she could never quite pinpoint exactly, just knew it got you bullied as a kid, alienated as a teen, and dumped at the altar as an adult. The worst part was that she tried to be normal sometimes. In fact, it was usually times when she thought she was managing to fit in the best that she got the strangest looks. Once a good friend had even commented, "You're so weird, Sophie"—literally on the heels of one of Sophie's "Hey, this is it. I'm being normal" moments of self-congratulation.

Sophie made a show of adjusting her bra strap as some other woman stepped into the bathroom hall maze. She didn't mind looking a bit socially inept, but she didn't want to be caught obviously eavesdropping. The woman disappeared as Sophie listened to what, if anything, Jesse would say to defend her. She restrained herself from crossing her fingers in pathetic hope by clenching her hands together. Was this what she'd sensed in him all night? Was this what was off? In private, just the two of them, he hadn't really noticed or minded her . . . uniqueness. But out here in the real world, as annoying people liked to call it (Good grief, every part of world was real, wasn't it?), did her weirdness send out some silent scream alert that only she didn't hear? It was no wonder she got on better with five-year-olds than most adults.

She leaned closer to the privacy screen to hear better, praying it wasn't see-through or her hulking shadow would be an embarrassment for the ages. She didn't need to strain; Jesse practically yelled his response.

"I know, Stella. I know."

"So why are you wasting your time?"

"I'm not 'wasting' my time. I'm getting to know someone who's pretty great, actually. Have you ever thought that maybe, just maybe, different is good? Is excellent even? Is exactly what suits me?"

Stella—whom Sophie sincerely regretted taking a liking to that first night—made a scoffing noise. "Please. Crystal was different from you too."

There was a soft pounding sound, like maybe Jesse hit the table. "It's not the same."

Stella must've raised her eyebrows or given him a pointed look or made some other silent commentary because Jesse sped on. "Look, I'm not rushing into anything. I promise. It's just nice to hang out with someone where there's no pressure. No commitment. We'll have a nice time, we'll part ways, life will go back to normal—except maybe I'll be a little less jaded, a little more open to the idea there's someone out there for me after all."

Hurt surprise crashed through Sophie, and she pushed her clenched hands against her mouth to keep from squeaking in pain. Already? In just a few hours he went from "then we'll make plans about how to see each other in the future" to "we'll part ways"? She should have known.

Oh, come off it. You already *did* know, a nasty voice—Kyle's—wheedled in her head.

Stella spoke again, sounding sad—which didn't make sense. Like she had any right to sorrow when she was being so, so . . . *mean.* "Wow, Jesse. You really are deluded. Of course there's someone for you. There has always been someone for you, and since you're ready to date again, maybe—"

"Excuse me? Can I help you, ma'am?" The voice and movement at Sophie's elbow stole her attention—and stopped Stella mid-sentence on the other side of the screen.

Sophie shook her head. "No, thank you. Sorry. I just—just got hit by a whopping headache." Unfortunately, it was true. Her skull was suddenly pounding.

She slipped around the screen and nodded at Stella. "Stella, we meet again."

"I didn't think you'd remember me," Stella said lightly, giving Sophie a full body scan as she took her seat.

"Oh, you're pretty memorable, even when a person's soused," Sophie said.

"Well . . . I should get back. It's hard for the staff to party without me, ha ha. Come by the pub tomorrow, Jesse. Celebrate New Year's with me. It's sold out, but I held back a ticket with your name on it."

Come by the pub, Jesse. Celebrate with me, Jesse, Sophie mimicked in her head, feeling juvenile and not in a good way.

"Yeah, yeah, I might, thanks," Jesse said, but his eyes were on Sophie.

He motioned at Stella's departing back with his thumb. "The pub staff has an annual get together between Christmas and New Year's."

"Why would I care?" Her words made his jaw drop—and fair enough. They kind of shocked her, too. "I heard . . . what you said," she continued.

He looked confused.

"You know. About having a nice time—"

He smiled.

"And parting ways, going back to 'normal.'"

The smile dropped from his face. "You don't understand. I wasn't—"

Sophie was suddenly very tired. "No, you're the one who doesn't 'understand.' Remember the toast I told you I made the night we met?"

Jesse nodded and his brow creased—and Sophie realized she was tuned in and mentally recording each of his micro responses to her every comment. She really was a freak. "And do you know why that's my resolution?" she pushed on, suddenly very recommitted to it.

Jesse shook his head again.

"Because I don't do this well. I try to mean the things I say. I don't play games—or not games with people anyway. You and your friend Stella are right, I guess. I am a weirdo. I spent a lot of years feeling bad about it—and then I stopped. I realized I'm fine. That maybe it's the rest of you that suck."

"That wasn't at all what I meant or what I was saying—" Jesse was cut off by a server delivering their main course. They thanked him by rote and ignored their plates.

Sophie slid the wrap she'd worn with her dress up over her shoulders. "I'm sorry, Jesse. Don't feel too badly for me. No matter how I'd started to get my hopes up about you, deep down I knew it was crazy to be falling for you. I'm leaving town in less than a week. You're right that things will end, and . . . " She couldn't make herself say it was okay. It wasn't okay. It was tragic. Heartbreaking. Even if it was totally stupid of her to think so after such a short time.

Jesse's eyes narrowed, his jaw hardened, and he shook his head again.

She wanted him to stop her, to reassure her as he'd done before, to say something like, "I'm falling for you too, but it's terrifying. That's why I was dismissive about us. I didn't want Stella complicating things or asking questions I can't answer about our future. Please don't give up on us yet. We'll figure it out."

But he didn't say those things. Instead, his voice was impossibly soft and bitterly sad. "That's what you use your truth-telling for, hey? To put up walls as sturdy as any of mine."

She didn't know how to respond, so she shrugged.

He looked deep into her eyes, as if he was searching for something, and then he slowly rocked forward a bit, as if nodding with his whole body. "You're right, of course. We'll just end up doing a number on each other—and I like you too much to hurt you, or to want to be hurt by you."

Sophie's breath caught painfully in her throat. She wanted to say, "Wait, no, wait, I'm an idiot," but she couldn't speak.

Jesse swallowed hard, then motioned at their untouched food, prime rib and gravy congealing on the plate, grilled vegetables cooling and looking flat and dull. "Are you going to eat?"

Sophie shook her head. "I'm not hungry. For once."

The joke thudded like dead weight between them.

Jesse nodded and beckoned for their server. "Can you pack these to go, please?" Then he looked at Sophie and back at his plate. "Actually, just hers. Thank you."

"No, no. I'm good, too. Thanks."

"Is there something wrong?" The server was talking about the food obviously, but Jesse nodded. "Not with the meal, but yes."

He handed the server a small wad of bills. "Good?"

The server counted and nodded. "Change, sir?"

"No, keep it."

Jesse strode from the table, even while the server

was thanking him for the generous tip.

Sophie followed Jesse out of the heat of the restaurant, and as they stepped into the parking lot, it was impossible not to see the difference a few hours had made. The sun had disappeared behind the mountains, and the shadows in the dreary lot were deep and impenetrable. Their silence as they drove back to River's Sigh was absolute.

Chapter 16

December 31

RAINBOW CABIN SOMEHOW FELT THE reverse of cozy now that Sophie had only awkward moments ahead of her with Jesse, but she was confident—if sad—about her decision to stop spending time with him. *You've only known him six days. Get over it!*

She pulled the quilt she'd borrowed from the bedroom more tightly around herself and tried, with growing frustration, to ignore her cellphone buzzing away on the coffee table. It kept ringing and ringing. The caller just wouldn't give up. That could only mean it was one person: Kate. She debated answering at all. Even considered turning her phone off. But she had promised to check in every other day or so, and it had been two days or more. Two days! It felt like months. Plus, Kate was a worrier. If Sophie didn't get in touch, she'd call their parents—and probably the police or something. Also, it was New Year's Eve. What kind of rat avoided their sister-slash-best-friend on New Year's Eve? A dejected, embarrassed rat, that's who.

She should not feel this despondent about parting with Jesse. She should not!

There was a blessed moment of reprieve—and then the phone buzzed anew. Dammit!

"Hello?" Sophie croaked.

"Are you all right? What's wrong with your voice? Are you sick? Why haven't you called me? I was about to send out a search party!"

See? The consummate worrier. Sophie chuckled in spite of herself, but turned mournful again almost immediately. "I did a stupid thing."

"You didn't!" Kate sounded horrified. Too horrified, come to think of it.

"Wait . . . I'm talking about Jesse and letting him wreck my holiday, maybe. What are you talking about?"

"I'm talking about Jesse, too," Kate informed her. "You didn't learn your lesson the first night and you slept with him, didn't you?"

"What? No." But man, she'd wanted to.

She poured out every new detail from the past few days, ending with the restaurant and what she'd overheard.

Kate's response stopped her cold. "If you're quoting him word for word, I don't hear anything that's a big deal. You're overreacting."

"What?"

"Seriously. Hear me out. He's talking with a friend who, big bitch or not, we can assume cares for him and feels entitled to meddle in his life. All he said was that he was aware of how things looked, maybe even how they are—and I don't believe he meant he didn't want to keep seeing you after you leave. He was just sparing himself an awkward, continuing lecture when you were due back any minute."

"You think?"

"Occasionally."

"Ha ha—but why didn't he just say that then?"

"Did you give him a chance?" Kate's voice was kind, but her words were a sharp barb and caught Sophie painfully. She hadn't given him an opportunity to explain the conversation or expand on what he'd meant, no. He'd started to try, but the food's arrival, then her own impatience to shore herself up, minimize pain, and save face intruded.

"Well, maybe not . . . but it's not like he tried very hard."

Sophie knew her defense was weak, and Kate's snort proved it. "I think you were waiting for a reason to kibosh the whole thing. You had a flash of bravery, but got cold feet when you left your bubble, as you put it, and were confronted by the idea that you might be pursuing something that could change your life, that has risk."

"Oh my, look at the time—"

"Not so fast, and don't even try to use your silly humor routine to get rid of me."

"Kate—"

"No, listen." Kate's voice softened. "I know Kyle tore your guts out. It's the opposite of something you would do—lead someone on, then turn on him in public. You mean the things you say and you expect the same courtesy from others."

Hmm, Sophie thought. I aim for that, yes, but do I actually succeed all the time? She remembered how she'd acted the first night they'd met. Was that honest of her? Well, the lust had been—but she'd totally acted out of character, had been misleading, and Jesse seemed to understand, hadn't held it against her. Then she thought of Jesse's stunned-then-hurt-then-angry face as she confronted him, but wouldn't let him get a word in edgewise.

Kate continued. "But this Jesse guy is the first man to light even a spark of interest in you since Kyle—and you seem to have fun together, he seems to genuinely like you, not some projection of who he thinks you are or what you could be. . . ."

"I don't know. I'm starting to think all romantic love is a lie, that it's always a fantasy, based on what we wish life could be if it ever worked out."

"You don't really believe that. You've always been the princess waiting for a prince to see past her finger-paint smeared clothes and idiosyncrasies. You've always wanted to find true love."

Sophie closed her eyes. "I don't want to get hurt again."

"I know you don't. I know. But what if keeping

everybody out for the rest of your life hurts you more?"

Sophie didn't say anything at first. Was Kate onto something? This whole evening, she'd felt so sure that breaking off whatever relationship had been forming between her and Jesse was the right thing to do. Now she was anything but.

"Look, Kate, thanks—but I can't talk anymore tonight, okay?"

Sophie could hear Kate's objections even though she didn't voice any aloud. "All right," she said finally. "Have a good night, okay? I love you."

"I love you too. I'll call again soon. Give Pete snuggles for me."

"Will do—and just a warning. The kids keep feeding him treats. I think he's gained five pounds."

Sophie shut her phone off and plugged it in to charge. The window revealed it had started snowing again. Big heavy flakes swirled in the black night, thoroughly hiding the lay of the land from Sophie's view.

Chapter 17

THE LIGHTS WERE ALL OFF at Maggie's, mercy of small mercies, even though it wasn't all that late yet. Jesse rolled to a stop by a thick ridge of frozen snow and gravel the plow had piled over the curb. Maggie had parked in the garage, and there was plenty of room in the driveway, but he figured the further he kept engine noise from her door, the better chance he had of going undetected.

He'd just opened the main door to the garage and stepped inside, sleds in tow, when a booming voice echoed off the cement around him. He practically jumped out of his skin. "You're back! I didn't expect you until tomorrow. How'd the date go?"

Maggie stood in the doorway to the house, framed by the mudroom's light that she'd just switched on.

Busted. Dang it. He hung the sleds on their designated nails and turned to face his sister's indomitable cheer. "I've had better."

She looked at him for a long moment. "Irish cream and cocoa it is then. Come in. Come in."

The drive to drop Sophie off after the dinner date

111

disaster had been excruciating. He was struck mute by a gut-roiling mix of anger, confusion, and hurt, and she was equally taciturn. He could understand how she'd misconstrued the conversation she'd overheard, but her overreaction and unwillingness to hear him out, to let him explain his side and say what he'd actually meant for flip's sake, reminded him so much of Crystal that he figured he should thank his lucky stars for the boot in the butt and the tip to stay clear. But if parting ways was the right choice, why did he feel so badly?

"Well?" Maggie asked, still haloed by the light. "Are you coming or not?"

"I'm coming. I'm coming—but make mine a double." He lumbered into the house behind his sister, feeling like he was carrying a four hundred pound weight. His body ached with memories of how the evening ended, and how he only had himself to blame.

"Well, you only have yourself to blame," Maggie said archly, an hour or so later, when the story of the past week was out on the table.

"I knew you'd say that. Heck, I just said that myself."

"What were you thinking? Anyone who takes someone home for the night the first time they meet and then changes her mind mid-screw has more than one or two bolts loose."

Jesse sighed, bone weary. How had he possibly thought talking with Maggie would help him? "You are totally, one hundred percent, missing the point. A person can change their mind about sex whenever they want, and I don't think it's her regular thing anyway—but again, that's not the point either. I really like her. Liked her? I don't know. It doesn't matter anyway."

"But what if you were a rapist? What if you didn't take her change of heart seriously?"

"Well, I'm not a rapist, and I did listen to her, of course, so that's moot—and I only told you about that night in the first place because I wanted to show the instant connection we had."

"Connection—pah," Maggie said. "Booze infused lust, more like it."

Jesse drained his cup. "Can you please get over the one night that didn't happen and say something to cheer me up or enlighten me, or just, I don't know—never mind. I'm going to go." He stood up.

"No, sit. Stay. Don't go. I'm sorry."

"I hate it when you talk to me like I'm your dog," Jesse grumbled, but he did sit again, mainly because his house was still a mess of torn up carpet and newly primed walls and he had less than no interest in returning to River's Sigh. He hadn't been able to bring himself to stay after he dropped Sophie off. Just waited, engine idling, for her to climb out of the truck in that sexy dress that had started the whole night to shit. Watched until she got into her cabin safely, then turned around in the driveway.

Maggie held the bottle out toward him and he nodded. She refilled their mugs—just milk and booze this time, no cocoa. Then she tightened the lid on the bottle and returned it to the highest shelf in her pantry. He'd asked her once, why she was such a stickler—two drinks maximum at one time, and never more than twice a month.

She had looked at him seriously, then smiled, though it didn't soften her eyes. "After Mark left I took to having wine every night after the kids went to bed. One day, it hit me . . . I wasn't yet, but I was well on my way to becoming a drunk. Like they need that on top of all the other crap they've been dealt."

Remembering that conversation and a million others covering the strict do's and do not's that Maggie lived by, Jesse realized that was part of her hang-up about the near one-night stand. She wasn't a prude, but she knew it would hurt him. They were cut of the same cloth, after all. Also, she refused to "run around" (her wording) or date very often because she didn't want to bring a slew of men around her kids, put them at risk, or have them start to care for one and then lose him too. He suddenly felt very fond—and very sorry—for his serious sister. The Ales kids hadn't been lucky in love, to say the least. He leaned forward and held his fist out to her.

She looked at him a minute, then laughed and lightly bumped his fist with hers. "Weirdo," she said.

"I know. You too."

"So one thing I don't get," she said a few minutes later.

"Uh huh?"

"You said something about how the minute you saw her dressed up, you knew things weren't going to go well at dinner."

Jesse crossed his arms. "It's just . . . well, every other time we hung out she was so laid back and cool and fun. She wasn't, like, putting on airs or anything."

"How is it 'putting on airs' to dress up for dinner?"

"You don't get it. She was gorgeous."

Maggie rolled her eyes. "Yep, being gorgeous. I see the problem."

Jesse stumbled over how to explain what he meant. "It's just—I don't know. She reminded me of Crystal: beautiful, polished, someone who turns a lot of heads. It made me realize how different we are. I can't offer what she needs or wants to be happy long term."

Flushed red circles appeared high on Maggie's cheekbones. She was angry, but why?

"So let me get this straight. You felt threatened because she looked too beautiful? You want some slobby hobbit girlfriend who's only comfortable at home or in private with you, attending to your every need?"

"No, wait—"

"No, *you* wait. I was happy when you said she was totally different from Crystal—but I didn't realize that you meant for all the wrong reasons. If anything, it sounds like you're looking for a dowdy version of Crystal. Someone who's weak-minded and insecure— you just erroneously think, apparently, that a dowdier version won't leave you."

"But—"

"No buts. What Sophie reacted to, what she over-heard that you said she'd misunderstood, was dead on. You got scared. She, of course, didn't hear the back-handed compliments, that you were sure she'd leave you because she's not only independent, quirky, and brave, she's beautiful. She only registered the fact that you were already planning to bail."

Jesse gritted his teeth and tried to hold back his rage. What was with the women in his life not letting him talk? He needed to work on that. "I never thought she was dowdy. She is the furthest thing from that, and I don't want—or need—her to need me. I want her to want me. For me to be enough for her, maybe for always."

Maggie made a surprised sound.

Jesse nodded. "I know, right?" He cracked his knuckles. "But tonight I saw her, not just through my eyes when we're alone and having fun, but through the eyes of everyone who stopped to talk to her, who wanted to meet her . . . and I heard her talk about her friends, her life in the city, the traveling she's done, and I just . . ." He shook his head. "Well, I just know that she needs, deserves, more than what I am or what I can give her. And *that*—even though Sophie's not at all like Crystal and it wouldn't be for the same reasons, specifically—is exactly what destroyed Crystal and me. I wasn't enough."

Maggie's eyes glistened and she looked away. "I'm sorry," she said finally. "I misunderstood you. I get it now—but for the record, I think you're totally wrong. I think you have everything to offer her. To offer anyone, actually."

Jesse cleared his throat. "You're my sister. You have to think that."

"I'm your sister, yep—which actually means I'm less prone to giving you the benefit of the doubt, as this conversation should prove."

"Yeah, I guess." He tried to laugh to ease the tension, but the sound wobbled like a badly damaged thing.

They each sipped their drinks. "You know I don't have any wisdom in the relationship department," Maggie said after a bit. "But there are some things you should think about before you let this Sophie woman go."

"Yeah, like what?"

"Well, she came for a holiday on her own, which suggests she's looking for something different from, or in addition to, her city life and the friends you're so insecure about. And for some weird reason, she obviously finds you wildly attractive—which is a bit gross, but you know, whatever."

Maggie's jibe worked and Jesse chuckled, sincerely this time. Her tone grew serious once more. "And she seems like a homebody. She loves children. And she's not hard to please—I mean, she likes tobogganing and building snowmen."

"When you put it like that, she does sound like the perfect woman," Jesse said, but he felt none of the joviality he forced into his tone.

"So what are you going to do about it, stud?"

It was a good question, but Jesse couldn't face it right now. He changed their conversation and asked about the best day and time to take the kids sledding as promised. Shortly after that, Maggie started yawning and brought him a blanket so he could crash on the couch.

Despite his exhaustion, however, sleep was a long time coming. Maggie's words scratched at him. Sure, Sophie seemed like the perfect woman for him—but he'd thought that about Crystal once upon a time, too. And his own last words to Sophie haunted him. "I like you too much to hurt you, or to want to be hurt by you."

And that was the unavoidable truth, wasn't it? And regardless of what bad things it said about him, it would remain the truth. He had thought, for a few brief days of fun delusion, triggered by their dreamlike retreat at River's Sigh, that maybe he could overcome his jaded weakness, but he couldn't. He had enjoyed moments of happiness the past few months—even before meeting Sophie—and he wouldn't risk being gutted again. He barely survived it the first time; he wouldn't get over it a second time.

Not from her.

Chapter 18

December 31

NEW YEAR'S EVE DAWNED COLD and clear. The snow that had started when Sophie was on the phone with Kate must not have meant business because the yard looked the same as when Sophie went to bed. The chilly periwinkle sky gave no sign of the storm the radio's local news was warning of.

Sophie spent the morning and early afternoon baking goodies and making appetizers. She had planned a New Year's party for one, after all, though maybe if things went according to the plan forming in her head—

She shut that thought off, whenever it popped up, not wanting to jinx anything. She did a poorer job of refraining from looking out across the white field of snow between her cabin and the big house. Jesse had left after dropping her off last night, and he hadn't come back. She shivered at the idea of being so thoroughly alone—and at the knowledge of what she was thinking of doing.

After a light lunch she took a long walk, revisiting the path and places she and Jesse had explored together. Even in the broad daylight her breath showed white in the air. It was definitely the coldest day since she'd arrived. She was also a little surprised at how spooky a place could feel in the middle of day. When her lungs hurt from exerting herself in the freezing air, and she realized—gross—that the weird feeling in her nose was her boogers freezing, she tramped her way back from the creek. And just in time. Two cars eased up the long driveway and into the parking lot. The rental car company, dropping off her car.

She thanked them profusely for the excellent service and waved as the man who'd delivered her car hopped into his coworker's vehicle and they departed. She already felt less intimidated by the wild emptiness, knowing she had wheels if she needed them. Still, she was proud of herself. She was honoring a new resolve: to do things even when they were scary. Sometime in the middle of the night, partially due to Kate's insights, no doubt, it had occurred to her that her resolution to be single was all wrong. She might still end up that way—and happily—but it wouldn't be out of fear. And on that note, it was time.

Jesse still hadn't shown up, but even if he didn't return to River's Sigh that evening, she had a clue about where he might be celebrating New Year's. Every fiber of her body hated the idea of confronting him with her true feelings in a public place where the chance he'd reject her equally publicly caused a nasty, crawling itch of déjà vu, but she felt she had no choice. She had no idea if he'd come back to River's Sigh. She'd told him she'd fend for herself for breakfasts. She'd arranged with Jo before coming that she'd do her own housekeeping. If she didn't track Jesse down tonight, she'd have no idea where to possibly find him, and she might have to leave town never knowing what, if anything, could have developed between them if she hadn't been such a coward.

She ate cold cuts on rye with hot mustard for dinner, and then ran a hot bubble bath, planning to get ready for the evening in a leisurely manner. A New Year's pub party wouldn't get started until later anyway. While she was waiting for the tub to fill, she called Kate.

"Happy New Year!"

Kate laughed. "Well, you're a little early, but it's sounding promising for you anyway, so that's good. I'm just bundling the kids up and getting ready to head to Mom and Dad's. What's up?"

Sophie paced back and forth with her phone and outlined her plan. "So what do you think? Am I insane to track him down in public and ask for another chance? It kind of feels like a potential repeat of me and Kyle, though not quite at the same level, of course."

"If Jesse is half the man you seem to think he is, he'll come through for you. He won't embarrass you or leave you hanging, I'm sure of it."

A buzz of warm happiness chased the last of Sophie's second thoughts away. Surely Jesse wouldn't let one bad night and a misunderstanding keep them from at least seeing where the rest of the week would take them? After all, he'd been a jerk their first breakfast together, and she'd heard him out and given him the benefit of the doubt.

"Okay!" She had to rein herself in so she didn't squeal like one of the kids in her class. "It's decided. Wish me luck!"

"You won't need it—but good luck."

"Have fun at Mom and Dad's. Give them and the kids hugs for me."

"You bet. Any New Year's resolutions you want me to share with the group?"

It was one of their family's big traditions. Usually they each made lists, actually. Sophie hesitated though. "Not this time," she finally said. "I think I want it to be a surprise."

"All right. I should run—and don't worry. Have fun tonight. I stand by my word. If Jesse is any kind of man, he'll be kind and over the moon for a second chance."

Sophie thought "over the moon" was a bit much, but she appreciated the vote of confidence and felt a lot more optimistic as she slipped into the yummy mango-scented bath.

It was almost ten o'clock when Sophie parked in

the closest spot she could get to the pub—one street over and a couple blocks away. As she walked and got closer, the pub's big glowing windows showed the party was in full swing, packed despite the intensifying cold. She hoped that Stella's words to Jesse—that the party was fully booked, no tickets available—was an exaggeration, aimed at pushing him to confirm he'd attend. If she couldn't get in, she didn't have a plan B.

Dress shirt and tie notwithstanding, the man who stopped her at the door was definitely a bouncer. He nodded pleasantly enough and held out his palm. "Ticket?"

"Uh." Sophie bit her lip. "Can I just buy one here?"

A head shake. "No, sorry. It was a pre-sold event."

"Oh, that's too bad. I'm from out of town and thought I had plans for the evening. I didn't even think to buy a ticket."

"I'm really sorry, ma'am."

Damn. The dratted ma'am again.

Sophie shrugged and smiled. "Ah, that's life, right? Have a good time tonight—and happy New Year's."

"You too, ma'am."

She started back to her car, wondering what to do next. Why on earth hadn't she and Jesse exchanged cell phone numbers? Who didn't do that in today's day and age? Was he on Facebook? Maybe she could message him that way—or, better yet, maybe she could find his sister's house again and track him down there. Why that seemed better than using Facebook she had no idea.

She was nearing her vehicle when someone ran up behind her. She inhaled sharply, but maintained her unhurried pace. The car was close. She hit the unlock button and the car flashed its lights and beeped.

"Excuse me, miss? Miss?" the runner, a male, called.

She was the only one on the dark street, so obviously she was the "miss" in question. She turned to face the stranger, not feeling particularly nervous, but looking for which nearby buildings had lights on and looked occupied, just in case.

"Sorry, are you talking to me?"

"Yes, thank you for stopping." A tall thin man with raven black hair and prominent nose closed the distance between them, panting lightly. "I was just talking to Brad, the bouncer. I got called into work and can't make the party, but the tickets are fifty bucks, so I came to see if they're refundable, but Brad said no—"

"But he pointed me out and said I might buy it off you?"

"Exactly."

"That would be perfect, actually. Thanks."

Sophie handed the man a fifty and received a glossy blue and ivory ticket in return. Then he was off and running again.

It was just after ten-thirty, but she was finally inside. Short of finding a staff member and asking to borrow their PA system or something, she was at a complete loss as to how to find Jesse in the huge crowd. Greenridge was such a small town and the pub had been so empty when she'd visited it, the notion it would be packed to the rafters hadn't even occurred to her.

She handed her red wool jacket to the coat check, and trying not to jostle other people—or get too jostled—she made her way toward the complimentary buffet table. (Well, complimentary in that it was included in the price of your ticket, anyway.) Holding her small plate, she scanned her surroundings for Jesse. As she did, she couldn't help but notice that she probably should've worn jeans. She wasn't the only woman in a skirt or dress, but she was the only one in an evening gown. Oh, well. She'd been going to wear it for her own party for one, so why not?

She poured herself a small cup of punch, planning to wait to order a drink until she found Jesse. *If* she found him, that is. She was usually fine in a crowd and comfortable attending events on her own, but tonight she felt conspicuous—as if the partying pub goers were a homogenous group and she wore a sign that said, "Not from here," across her chest. Still, she knew better than to take it personally, or did until she overheard a bizarre conversation between two women, who appeared to be staring at her.

"I think that's her. Actually, I'm sure it is. Who else would it be?" the brunette said.

"*Bitch*," her friend, a redhead with sharp, pinched

125

features, agreed.

Sophie glanced over her shoulder, looking for the object of the gossip, but there was no one directly near her or obviously singled out. A big group crowded the pool tables. A smaller group was trying to get some dancing going. She was the only person in direct line of the women's stare down.

And then the comments got even stranger, but also a lot clearer.

"I don't know what Jesse sees in her. Stella's totally right. She's nowhere close to Crystal's league. She's not even in *Stella's* league. I mean, she's pretty enough, if you like that look—but she's kind of fat."

The redhead snickered. "Yeah, I can't believe Stella's waited all this time for him to get off his ass—and now *that's* the ass he wants."

The two vipers laughed at their cleverness, and Sophie's cheeks lit on fire—but she wasn't altogether unhappy at what she'd overheard. It explained Stella's change toward her. She'd been nice enough until Jesse showed an interest in her. Stella was obviously hoping that with Crystal out of the picture, she'd have a chance with Jesse. She had a thing for him. Interesting.

She beamed a smile at the two women and strode toward them. "So you guys know Stella and Jesse?" she asked. "*Perfect.* I'm looking for either one of them, have you seen them?" Their stunned expressions made her want to laugh her head off, but she managed to keep a straight face.

"Uh," the brunette said.

Pinchy-face hemmed and hawed. "Um, I'm not sure. . . ."

Sophie decided to have one more bit of fun. She popped a cube of cheese from her plate into her mouth and made an exaggerated Mmm sound. "So good," she exclaimed. "*Soooo* good."

Brunette and Pinchy-face exchanged glances. "I'm sure Stella's in the kitchen. I don't—" The dark-haired woman shrugged and actually looked apologetic. "Well, I'm not sure Jesse's even here, if he's even coming, I mean."

"Thanks for your help," Sophie said, meaning it. "You've been very kind." The last line, she'd admit it, was a little less sincere.

Sophie was almost at the big swinging gate that led to the kitchen, thinking she'd park herself outside it and just wait, when hinges creaked nearby. An exterior exit to her left swung open violently. A gale force of icy air blasted in, and a blur of color burst through the door. It was Stella, dressed to the nines in turquoise, pink in the face, but looking upset, so Sophie wasn't sure if the heightened color was from the cold or from high-running emotion.

Stella stopped dead when she saw Sophie. "How did you get in here?"

Sophie opened her mouth to explain the ticket, but Stella cut her off, her expression changing slightly, though Sophie wouldn't say it softened exactly. She couldn't tell what was going on behind Stella's dark eyes at all.

"You're here for Jesse."

It wasn't a question, but Sophie nodded anyway, relieved that she wasn't going to have to ask Stella about him.

Stella sucked in her lips, studying Sophie, then looked her in the eye. "Well, good luck."

Rats, she *was* going to have to ask. "Do you know where I can find him?"

Stella only hesitated a second. "Well, when we last chatted, he was outside catching a breath of air. I think he came back in, though. He has a table by the stage."

Sophie glanced toward the door that had banged shut after Stella's frenzied entry. Stella and Jesse had been outside together? Had their conversation somehow upset Stella, or was Sophie just imagining things?

"I have to run," Stella said. "I've got a shit ton of drinks to serve."

"Yes, of course. Have a good time tonight. Happy . . . New Year."

Stella huffed and rushed off, but Sophie caught her departing comment, "Oh, yeah, it'll be fantastic. Bloody fantastic."

It was still hard for Sophie to link this Stella with the one she'd met her first night in town and she felt kind of bad. She'd obviously stepped in the middle of Stella's hopes and plans or something, but good grief, she hadn't meant to. And Jesse sure didn't seem to have any reciprocal interest in Stella. He'd only ever mentioned her in passing, the same way he'd spoken of other Greenridge friends and inhabitants when they chatted.

She deposited her empty plate in a bin on a nearby cart and tried not to white knuckle her punch glass as she made her way toward the stage, keeping an eye out for tall bearded men who might be Jesse.

She'd only made it as far as the dance floor when Stella appeared at her elbow again, carrying a tray of empty beer steins. "Look, Sophie, I only have a minute, but I wanted to say I'm sorry."

"Oh?"

Stella's chin bobbed. "Yeah. I ran into Carrie and Viv, friends of mine, and I figure you know about me and Jesse."

"Not really. Is there something to know?"

"No, no—just wishful thinking, I guess. Anyway, I wanted to apologize for being such a cow."

"You weren't that bad. It's fine."

"Okay, well, thanks." Stella went to move past Sophie, then turned back. "Maybe it's not my place to say this, but Jesse really likes you."

Sophie's heart raced, but she tried to keep looking calm.

"But, well, he's really angry. I don't know if he'll talk to you."

"Did he say that?" The words flew from Sophie's mouth before she could stop them.

129

Stella bit her lip. "Something like that—and that he's tired of being the one always out on a limb, taking all the risks."

That didn't really sound like Jesse. If anything, he'd say the opposite, that he had stopped taking risks, that he hadn't chanced anything in years. They'd both admitted that.

Stella was talking again, but Sophie realized she hadn't heard a word. "What? Sorry, pardon me."

Stella waved her free hand, the tray still aloft in the other. "You're probably not interested anyway, but I've known Jesse a long time. He loves grand gestures, big shows of affection." She paused as if waiting for an answer. "Oh, you really didn't hear me. I said there's going to be an open mic thing, starting—" she glanced at the big clock above the bar, "in about seven minutes and going until the countdown. It's sort of tradition here, got started a couple years ago as a joke, but then it really caught on and people always ask for it."

"An open mic?"

"Yeah, you know, a chance to share any special thanks, moments, or regrets about the past year and to make wishes for the new one."

Sophie's heart pounded so loudly she was sure Stella would hear it over the bass hammering from the sound system. It had been hard enough for her to decide to track Jesse down in public in the hopes of making amends or getting him to give them another go, knowing that if he declined, she'd have to run a gauntlet of strangers while trying to mask her disappointment. Even if none of them knew her or noticed her, it would be hard enough. But to stand up in front of a crowd and ask him for another chance? Every part of her screamed *no*.

But her mind filled with Jesse's kind eyes and gentle smile—and his endearing awkwardness.

And suddenly she felt sure this was the right thing to do. She'd done an abrupt turn in the week she'd been here, going from vowing to avoid all risk of hurt by staying single to being willing to face potential pain in order to live fully and be honest with herself. Saying aloud, here and now, what she hoped, what she wanted, would be a very good first step.

Plus, like an omen she was doing the right thing, Kate's encouraging words came back to her. *If Jesse is half the man you seem to think he is, he'll come through for you. He won't embarrass you or leave you hanging, I'm sure of it.*

"Okay," she said to Stella. "I'm in. Where do I sign up, or is it first come, first served?"

Stella looked surprised. Then she grinned. "There's a sheet on the table by the DJ's booth."

Chapter 19

JESSE TRACED THE RIM OF his glass. The drink was pretty much finished, just slinking cubes of melting ice remained. He'd been stupid to come tonight. He'd counted on the noise and bustle to distract him from thinking, but it was the reverse. Every laugh underlined the fact he had no one to share a smile with. Every rumble of chat and conversation highlighted that he was alone and silent. And every drink, raised or poured, reminded him of Stella's bizarre confession—and painfully prodded the tender obsession that every thought centered on or circled back to: Sophie.

Stella wanting to "be with him," to "see where things might go"? Stella "having a thing for him," even before Crystal was in the picture? It was like suddenly finding out the moon wasn't the moon at all or that the sun was an illusion.

"I just thought, once you healed up from Crystal, we'd finally have our chance," Stella had said—but even as she looked up at him in the dim glow of the streetlight, it wasn't her face he saw. It was Sophie's. Just like it was Sophie's voice he'd wanted to hear saying the words that Stella spoke—except now he knew that would never happen.

He had told Stella the truth, that she was great, more than great, but that he'd never, not even once, thought of her as anything more than good-buddy-Stella. His feelings for her were pretty much exactly like his feelings for Maggie.

To say Stella had been unhappy with that response was putting it mildly. Furious was more apt.

"Is it because of Sophie?" she'd asked.

He considered that before answering. Was it because of Sophie? He'd never thought of Stella romantically, true, but if some small corner of his being wasn't hanging onto hope that he and Sophie might continue, would he at least entertain the possibility of dating Stella? He didn't think so.

He shook his head. "I'm sorry." And he had been. He was.

Stella's face tightened into a rigid mask; he almost didn't recognize her. "Well, good, because you don't have a snowball's chance in hell with her."

He reeled back like she'd slapped him and she looked glad. "Why do you think I tried to stop you from going with her that first night, you dummy? And why do you think I tried to intervene, make you see sense at the restaurant yesterday?"

"I don't know . . . because you wanted you and me to get something going, not me and Sophie?"

Stella practically spat, her eyes sparking fire, and

though she only wore a pretty green dress—probably for his benefit, he realized with growing unhappiness—she hadn't seemed cold. She seemed about to explode. "Only half right. Regardless of what I might have wanted for me. I want what's good for you—and that's not her. People always yammer at me when they're drunk, and she was more than clear about what she wanted for her little vacation: a cute guy for a holiday lay or two before she moved on."

"But we didn't even—I mean, we haven't . . ."

Stella's eyes widened at the confession and she inhaled deeply as if considering the significance of his words. "Ah, and that explains the rest."

"What rest?"

"Well, Carrie, trying to be friendly, recognizing her from my descriptions, started chatting with her and asked about you guys and she was like, 'Jesse who?' It confused Carrie, and when she said she thought you guys were seeing each other, Sophie just laughed and said, 'Yeah, that'll never work out.'"

Even now, nursing another gin, thankfully delivered by a server other than Stella, recollections of their conversation felt like physical blows. And a sudden realization hit him with horrible clarity. He'd been lying to himself when he'd decided at Maggie's that he wasn't going to pursue Sophie anymore. He couldn't give her up so easily. Besides, there was something not quite right in Stella's report about what Sophie supposedly said. Then again—ah, forget it. It was too much to think about right now. Everything was too much.

A voice crackled over the PA, asking people to order pre-countdown drinks and to sign up for the stupid open mic. Maybe he'd hit the road before that got started. It was true that he hadn't pined for Crystal in a long while now, but the open mic would probably still stir memories he'd like to avoid. At the very least, it would be a painful reminder of how most things with her, even their "love," was a merely a big show.

He'd always craved cozy, intimate New Year's celebrations—a time to reflect on the past and plan and dream for the future. She always wanted to party. Less than a week before she left him for a guy she'd been sleeping with for six months—that half of Greenridge knew about, even if he had no clue—she'd made the gloppiest, most overtly sentimental open mic toast to him ever seen. And, of course, he'd eaten it up—even as he'd wondered why anyone would put someone they cared about on the spot like that.

Chapter 20

WAS IT A BAD IDEA or a great one? Sophie couldn't fully decide, yet she stood in the haphazard line up, getting bumped this way and that by other eager participants. Either way, it was probably too late—well, no, it wasn't. She could duck out. They'd call her name a couple times and move on. But she felt committed now, like she'd be failing herself if she didn't go through with it.

She barely heard the chatting and laughter around her, she was so focused on figuring out what to say—something that conveyed the depth of her feelings, but that wasn't too over-the-top personal and mushy. She didn't want to mortify Jesse to death.

There was a huge explosion of clapping and cheering, and a young blonde held her hand up in the air, showing off a ring she'd just received. A blushing, beaming boy held the mic. That solidified it. If someone could propose in front of a crowd like this, she could say how much fun she'd had with Jesse, express that she hoped it continued, and wish him a happy New Year either way—

Her name was called.

She approached the mic with legs of lead and a heart of butterflies, but as soon as her hand closed around the slightly damp foam handle, her nerves calmed and her classroom persona kicked in, the Sophie who led assemblies and wrangled crowds of parents and students and staff at endless you-name-it functions.

She hadn't set eyes on Jesse yet, and staring out into the noisy crowd, she wondered if Stella had lied. Maybe he wasn't there—and then she found him, glass in hand, somehow managing to look completely isolated in the boisterous chaos. Why did he hang out here so often when he seemed to prefer alone time? Another question to ask someday. He looked up and their eyes met. She smiled and waggled her eyebrows, straining to send him a telepathic message: I'm so sorry. He didn't appear to receive it. His forehead creased. She realized the crowd was getting restless. She'd better speak her piece.

"I'm new to Greenridge," she started.

Someone hooted and another person yelled, "Welcome."

She didn't bother to explain she was just visiting. Keep to the relevant bits, she lectured herself. "And it's gorgeous, just gorgeous—the prettiest place I've ever seen." More approval from the crowd. "But when I arrived, I was feeling jaded and bruised. I'd written off romance for good."

"Preach it, sister!" hollered a very large, very drunk shiny-haired brunette at a nearby table. "Love sucks!"

Sophie—and the roomful of listeners—laughed. "And I can't say I've found love, but I did meet a really nice guy who has sort of restored my belief in the whole silly notion."

"Awwwwwww," the packed pub chorused as one.

"I know, I know. So corny, right?" She inhaled deeply. "Anyway, I treated this guy a little badly—or at the very least, unfairly."

"Oh, no, you didn't!" The brunette was on a roll, and the crowd roared again.

Sophie nodded. "Yes—and I shouldn't have. I should've heard him out. And I'd like to say I'm sorry and ask for another chance."

She was aware of the crowd all around her, but only in a peripheral sense. It was as if nothing separated her from Jesse, who was burning her with a cold, unreadable stare. What had she done? Not a trace of a smile softened his expression. He looked like he wanted to stand up and rage.

She had to finish, though. She couldn't wimp out now.

"So what about it? You know who you are." Her voice had gone soft, so soft—but it seemed to boom through the speakers.

A rapt silence spread, yet Jesse still gave no sign that he even knew she meant him. The word, almost a beg, slipped from her lips and saline heat burned in her sinuses. "Please?"

All around her, heads turned this way and that, searching for a clue to the identity of the man to whom she spoke. She waited a heart beat longer—and then more. Still nothing.

"Okay, well, you know where I live." She bobbed her head once and smiled out at the crowd. "Well, that's all she wrote for this girl. Thanks for listening. May you each find love or something better—chocolate, maybe—in the New Year."

The crowd went wild. "Hear, hear!"

Jesse's dead-eyed expression didn't crack, but Sophie's heart felt like it did as she handed off the mic. She kept smiling and accepted some high fives from the crowd. Stella was right about one thing. This crowd loved them an open mic. Somehow she managed not to bolt—even as Jesse got to his feet and forced his way through the tide of bodies in the exact opposite direction of where she stood.

A new speaker took the floor. Sophie added to the applause at the end of the latest entreaty, not a lot different than hers had been, actually, then escaped. She retrieved her coat from the empty checkroom and fled through the exit Stella had revealed earlier.

Eleven fifty-seven. Three minutes to a whole new year. Hooray.

Chapter 21

New Year's Day

ALL IN ALL, IT WASN'T the worst New Year's Eve she'd ever had, Sophie thought as she surveyed the two empty wine bottles and remnants of destroyed appetizers and sweets. Her ill-fated wedding had taken place on New Year's Eve, too, after all. Bizarrely, the coincidence made her chuckle. Maybe she was, finally, really over Kyle completely—a good thing, even if it did chafe that the most annoying "condolence" people heaved at her in the early days after their break up had proven true. "One day you'll laugh at this," they'd said—and here she was. Even if her laughter was only because she realized now, after forever burning her chances with a guy who really seemed right for her, how wrong for her Kyle had been all along.

She ate a mini cheesecake, then wrapped the rest of the plate and put it in the fridge. How on earth could she have thought that stupid mic idea was a good one? Oh, well. It didn't matter. She didn't regret it. She wouldn't let herself. She'd taken a shot and missed, hard core. But at least she hadn't chickened out. It did leave her at a conundrum in terms of her New Year's resolution, though. Maybe she'd try to adopt a less all or nothing approach.

She lifted her big glass of water. "To being single. Or maybe sometimes not." She swallowed an extra strength ibuprofen. The toast felt like it needed something. "Amen!"

Was that the upside to this whole new, confusing heart mess? In figuring out that she'd somehow fallen for Jesse—only to lose him—she'd learned she could care again. She could take risks.

Nah, that sounded like alcohol talking. She was probably still buzzing a little.

She went to the living room window and cracked the blinds that she'd closed when it felt like the long dark night was staring in at her—and gasped.

The sky had opened sometime after midnight and let down snow like she'd only ever seen in pictures. Where was the cabin's porch? Her car? Nowhere to be seen. She was more than awed. She was astounded. She went to the door and opened it carefully. Snow, almost to her chest, decorated with the imprint of the door—complete with a hole from the doorknob—greeted her. She shut the door. Locked and dead bolted it. (As if that was even necessary!) Then she ran to the side window and opened that blind, too. Darn! Just as she feared, her snow people had been obliterated.

The reality of her situation sank in. She was alone

out here, really alone.

She resorted to her favorite form of stress reduction other than food: self-talk. There's no need to panic, she lectured. No need. You could live here for weeks. You have plenty of food and water—and a phone. Right. The phone!

She grabbed her cell. No service.

She dug around for the cordless landline, grateful that Jo and Callum had thought to put phones in, even if initially she had thought that was "quaint."

What? Was this a joke? The phone lines were dead too? She looked out at the miles and miles of snow and guessed that made sense. She took technology for granted, almost like it was magic—but it was a service, and she couldn't imagine what kind of havoc a dump of snow like this would wreak.

She thought of Jesse. He'd know what to do. But she'd listened and watched for him—casually, of course—until she went to bed around three in the morning. She was sure he hadn't come back to River's Sigh.

So . . .

Nothing came to her. No improvised plan. No scheme. No craft.

She cleaned up the evidence of her party for one. She'd sit tight for a while, wouldn't panic.

Would try not to panic.

Chapter 22

ALL OF JESSE'S THOUGHTS WERE of Sophie—as they had been all night, or really, even before that, for days, but especially now. He could kick himself for being a fool. He hadn't had a lot to drink, just three over the whole evening. He would've been fine to drive, but no, because he had his knickers in a knot and didn't know what he was feeling or what he should do and wanted to avoid Sophie until he did know something, he'd couch surfed at Maggie's again. He'd planned to head out early to make Sophie breakfast and try to explain himself and beg her to forgive him for ignoring her like that. It was just that she'd caught him so off guard. And he was so friggen awkward in social situations anyway. But to publicly apologize and toast him on the heels of his thoughts about hating it when Crystal did the same thing? What were the chances of that?

"Slim to none," Maggie had informed him, repeating it for emphasis, "Slim to *none*. Stella put Sophie up to it somehow, knowing it wouldn't go over well."

He agreed. In fact, he'd arrived at that conclusion himself, even before he spilled the evening's events

143

over cheese and crackers at one a.m. He just hadn't figured out what he was going to do about it—and right now, his lame heartsickness over Sophie and how he might've accidentally hurt them beyond repair by failing to act, failing to respond to her, was the least of his concerns. She was alone in the bush, the highways were closed to vehicular traffic on both sides of River's Sigh, and there was another heavy snowfall warning in effect.

She was unusually comfortable left to her own devices in a pretty wild habitat, sure, but being completely cut off from the world was disconcerting even to people who lived here and expected it from time to time. And what if she got hurt and needed medical care or something? What the hell could he do? How could he get through to her?

Chapter 23

AT FIRST SHE THOUGHT THE distant buzzing roar was a helicopter. But the sound was wrong. And it wasn't coming from overhead. Or didn't seem to be. In the absence of other noise and with the extreme sound-dampening quality of all that snow, it was hard to tell. And then she thought it was a chain saw, or multiple chain saws. That made her sick and afraid, really afraid, for the first time. What kind of weirdo would be using a chain saw in weather like this? A psycho weirdo, that's who.

"Now you're just being stupid," she said aloud. "If someone wanted to murder you, they wouldn't have waited until there was five feet of snow to wade through."

She moved window to window throughout the cabin, straining to see anything, anything at all. Nothing. Just a blinding white backdrop met her every stare.

So where was the noise coming from? Was it getting louder? What did an avalanche sound like? Surely, though, River's Sigh B & B, however nestled in the mountains, wasn't built in an avalanche area? She shivered, but couldn't quite bring herself to stop uselessly fretting while she studied the otherworldly scene.

It wasn't even two in the afternoon yet, but it was like the day had cracked dawn and started an immediate descent into night. It hadn't really gotten light—just shifted to gray, lighter gray and back into darkening grays. And the snow. So much snow. She was caught in a children's picture book gone wrong.

She put a big kettle of water on to boil, trying to pretend it was just a regular day in her purposely-sought-after remote vacation. She tried to ignore the alarmed voice in the back of head that kept shrieking, What the hell were you thinking?

"It will be fine," she whispered to self-soothe. "You will be fine."

The kettle screamed just as the cutting-buzzing roar outside intensified. She jumped. Forcing herself to take a couple deep breaths, she poured the steaming water over two tea bags in a large pot to steep. Then—slowly, no running—she allowed herself to go and peer out the window. Again.

Two whirring black blurs, kicking up powder and spray, rocketed into view in front of the main house. They looked like massive snow-spitting beetles or scorpions. She squinted at them—and suddenly knew what they were. Snowmobiles. She'd heard of them, even had seen them on TV, just didn't have any personal experience with them.

The machines inched closer. And now that she knew what the noise was, she was less nervous, though her belly still fluttered a bit. Who rode the machines and what did they want?

Maybe Jo and Callum had seen a weather report and called people to have them check on her? Maybe Jesse had sent someone?

Jesse. That's who—and what—she really wanted. Jesse to show up, to say he would forgive her cowardice at the restaurant and the faux pas at the pub—to have them turn this freaky storm into the best story for future grandkids ever.

The thought hit her like a brick. *Future grandkids.* That meant she'd actually envisioned, or hadn't ruled out, kids. With Jesse anyway. Why had they always been off the table when she was with Kyle? And why hadn't she figured out all this at the restaurant during that stupid dinner, before it was too late?

The whirring was thunderously loud now. The mechanical bugs ate up the path between the parking lot and Rainbow cabin like it was nothing.

Just feet from where her porch lay buried, both engines halted, all noise cut out, and two tall, lumpy figures bundled in snowsuits and helmets, hopped off their rides—sank almost to their waists—and reached to unstrap snow shovels from their seats.

One of the incognito rescuers raised an arm and waved.

She mimicked the movement, then wrapped her

147

arms around herself and watched the snow fly as shoveling began.

Now that she was rescued, Sophie almost forgot she'd been afraid at all. Her mind was full of Jesse. What if he was one of the helpers? What if he wasn't? She could hardly hope—but she definitely couldn't keep from hoping.

Chapter 24

A GOOD HOUR LATER, THE two well-wrapped visitors stomped their boots on the freshly cleared porch. And then someone knocked—like it was necessary. Sophie opened the door wide before the gloved fist could lower to the wood a second time.

"Come in, please—and thank you! I made food and there's hot tea, or something stronger if you want it."

One snowman entered. The other shook his helmeted head. His voice was unfamiliar. "Thanks, but I'd better head out." He glanced up at the turbulent clouds and the sky that was readying for a new bombardment of white stuff. "I want to get back before all the light's gone."

The snowman in front of her, shedding leaves of snow from his vinyl suit in the cabin's warmth, nodded his masked and goggled face. "Sounds good, buddy. And thanks a lot, hey?" It was a voice Sophie recognized and her stomach flipped hearing it.

"No problem." The departing man gave a farewell salute and covered the ground back to his machine in easy strides, though Sophie noticed the cleared path was already filling in.

The door shut.

Sophie pressed her hands together and held them to her mouth, prayer-like. The man before her removed his goggles, soft black face mask, and helmet. It was, of course, Jesse. That she'd already known it was didn't keep her from making a happy surprised sound.

"You came for me."

"Well, like you said—I know where you live." His voice was as soft as hers, but then his warm eyes crinkled. "Besides, I'm being paid to take care of things around here. I think I owe you breakfast."

"I'm sorry about last night." She shook her head. "It was a lot of pressure."

"No, I'm the one who's sorry. You caught me by surprise, and I—never mind."

"No, what?"

"I'm going to say a lot of things to you, but there's something I want to do first."

"Oh, yeah? And what's that?" Sophie knew though, and she was lifting her face to his even as he put one arm around her waist and pulled her close.

The snow on his suit melted between their connected bodies, soaking Sophie's knit shirt. She shuddered, but not with cold.

His lips were icy, his tongue warm. Her body buzzed at the sensation of his beard against her skin, somehow both prickly and soft at the same time.

Time dissolved as quickly as the snow, and Sophie

was suddenly very, very glad for the storm.

"I can't think of a better way to spend New Year's Day," she said a little breathlessly when they eased apart. He didn't let her go, just kept his hands lightly on her hips.

"And how's that? Snowed in?" He grinned.

"Exactly."

"I'm glad too," he said, sounding a little shy despite the kiss they'd just shared. He searched her eyes. "I feel like we really have something—or could have something. I wish you'd met me before I was gun shy. I would've swept you off your feet. I would've been bold from the get-go—"

"You actually were pretty bold at the get-go if I recall," she said.

He laughed. "You know what I mean."

"I do." She nodded. "But it's not too late. I have feet. You can still sweep—"

She shrieked when he grabbed her up and did just that, depositing her in a lump on the couch, then stood, bracing himself one hand against the wall, and wedged off each heavy boot. When he pulled off his one-piece snowsuit, he was wearing red long underwear. She burst out laughing and couldn't stop.

"What?" he asked with mock hurt. "Why are you laughing?"

"Those are simultaneously the silliest and maybe the sexiest undergarments I've ever seen."

"You think silly and sexy can exist together?"

"Well, maybe not all the time, but definitely sometimes."

He cocked an eyebrow and grinned. "Then you're in luck. You should see an erection in these bad boys. It's hilarious."

She laughed. "I'd like to."

"Well, fair's fair—maybe if you show me your skivvies."

She bit her bottom lip and winked. "Oh, I plan to show you more than that."

He grinned.

"But maybe not yet. Not until we, you know, know for sure . . ."

Jesse sobered immediately and took her hand, entwined her fingers through his, and kissed each one of her knuckles. Then he sank down beside her on the couch. "I want nothing more than to spend the next five days ravishing you, but I agree."

She sighed. "I want that too, so much."

"But what I have in mind for us, what I really, really want, doesn't demand any hurry. I don't want you to freak out—don't freak out, okay?"

"Okay . . . "

"I see us together for the long haul, like, maybe the forever haul."

"*Haul*, hey? When you put it like that, it's so romantic."

His eyes creased so deeply they became slits.

Sophie lifted his arm, pulled it over her shoulder,

and snuggled in tight against him. "I have a friend who went to a one-week teaching convention and met a guy there. They were inseparable for the week, and he begged her not to leave, but she had to be sensible, so of course she did. And then she was back in six weeks and they were married in twelve. I thought they were insane."

"Uh huh . . ." Jesse hadn't shifted, hadn't moved away. His cheek was a gentle pressure on the crown of her head.

"Does that scare you? Do you think it's nuts or that I'm nuts for bringing it up?"

"Not at all. My mom and dad were happy every day of their married lives, except for the normal days every marriage has when they weren't."

Sophie smiled.

"And they met at a grad party and married in under six months. My sister and me? Neither of us married high school crushes. We each knew our spouses for months before we even dated. Were together for a sensible two and three years respectively before saying I do, yet both our marriages crashed and burned. We felt extra duped, like we'd been blind, been tricked, had never really known them."

"Yeah, that's how I felt, too. Maybe that's how it always feels."

Jesse was rubbing a soft figure eight shape up and down her forearm. "Yeah," he agreed.

"So maybe it all comes down to who you marry

and a bit of the luck of the draw, not how long you've known each other or how old you are or any of the other things people like to hold up as talismans to guarantee success."

They were comfortably silent a few minutes. Then Sophie noticed Jesse was shivering. She retrieved the blanket wedged under a couch cushion, tucked it around him, and went to fetch tea.

"And you're sure my story about my friend wasn't too psycho? You're not scared of me now?"

"Terrified. Totally."

She smacked him lightly, then handed him a steaming mug.

He thanked her and took a sip. "I guess I should tell you, just in case you're overly hopeful. I didn't bring a ring with me or anything. Just saying."

"Ha ha." Her face hurt with smiling. "Why don't you hurry up and get warm so we can do something interesting?"

"How interesting?"

"Pretty interesting, but maybe not *fully* interesting."

"I'm completely intrigued and warmer already. Does it involve me getting to see what kind of underwear you've got on under this?" He toyed with the hem of her shirt, then ran his cold hand under it, up and over her warm flesh, along the curve of her ribcage until he cupped one satin-clad breast.

"It could, if you wanted."

"What a happy coincidence. I do want. Pink like before?"

She shook her head and raised her eyebrows coquettishly. "Purple and—"

"Like it matters," he said. The tea was placed on the coffee table.

Outside the snow continued to fall, and the happiness Sophie felt was like a glowing warm ball, something tangible, something touchable, nameable, visible. "I don't want to go back to real life," she whispered.

"What are you talking about?" he whispered back. "This *is* our real life."

Epilogue

THE MINISCULE CHURCH WAS BARE and plain and chilly, yet somehow perfectly decorated and cheery with just one bouquet of fresh cut daffodils. And although it would hold about nine guests in the tiny pews, for now it held only Jesse, Kate, Maggie, and Pete, sitting on his graying haunches, decked out in a satin vest that held two rings, looking very noble as the ring bearer.

"I still can't believe you guys are doing this. It's been what, three months?" Kate whispered.

Jesse grinned at his soon-to-be sister-in-law. "Four—but we were waiting for each other forever. We just didn't know it yet."

Kate groaned and his own sister punched him. He read Maggie's sibling shorthand loud and clear. "I know. I love you too."

She snorted. "You forgot the 'even though you're corny as heck' bit that I thought first."

Kate giggled and he laughed, but the sound was cut short as Sophie, his Sophie, walked into the church on the arm of the pastor they'd arranged last minute.

The setting, the venue, the ceremony—and the people about to say "I Do"—couldn't have been any different from either of their first walks down the aisle.

"I love this," she breathed to him when the pastor deposited her at his side. "And I love you."

She'd been wide-eyed and stressed when he proposed—not about agreeing to marry him, thankfully, but at the notion of planning another big wedding. Even the first time, a huge affair hadn't been her idea. When he suggested the tiny deserted chapel on a remote part of the highway near River's Sigh B & B, it was like he'd offered to hang the moon for her.

"I hope he hurries up," she stage whispered about the pastor, who grinned good-naturedly. "I can't wait for the honeymoon."

Jesse couldn't either. They had two planned, actually. One right away and short, just the weekend, in Rainbow cabin at River's Sigh B & B—then a longer stint in the summer, when Sophie was finished her school year and free to move.

"You don't have to move. I'll move," he insisted multiple times, not eager to leave Greenridge, but willing to, absolutely.

She'd been equally vehement. "No way. I love my job, but my class changes every year anyway." Her next words would be forever seared in his heart. "Besides, coming here to you was like coming home. Forever."

"Are you ready?" the pastor asked.

Sophie giggled like a kid, and Jesse felt every last brittle part in his heart crack wide open. "We are," he said. "We totally are."

Dear Reader,

I hope you enjoyed *One to Keep* as much as I enjoyed writing it. River's Sigh B & B is my own dream getaway, and the more time I spend there, the more time I want to spend there. If you feel the same and the series is new to you, I hope you'll check out the other books: *Wedding Bands*, *Hooked*, *Spoons*, *Hook, Line & Sinker*, *Silver Bells*, *Reeling*, and *The Catch*.

And before I go, a fun little F.Y.I. The town I live in occasionally gets the kind of crazy snow that Sophie experiences for the first time. The winter before I started *One to Keep*, in less than twenty-four hours, my family's vehicles were completely buried and indistinguishable as even being cars!

Wishing you love, laughter and cozy nights,
Ev

P.S. I'd be honored if you'd like to connect. Please visit www.evbishop.com, where you can sign up for my newsletter, and/or find me on Facebook, follow my Twitter feed (Ev_Bishop), or drop me a line at evbishop@evbishop.com. I'd love to hear from you! And on a similar note, reviews really help authors. If you'd be so kind as to leave a few words on Amazon, GoodReads, your blog, Facebook, or anywhere else you hang out when your nose isn't in a book, I'd be very grateful.

Not ready to leave River's Sigh B & B yet? I never am either. Lucky for us, another romantic getaway awaits! Catch a peek of THE CATCH by reading on . . .

159

Chapter 1

MOTHER NATURE WAS AS BUSY revamping as the rest of the staff at River's Sigh B & B. Everywhere Aisha looked as she walked the trail to Minnow cabin, a lush green had replaced the dingy gray-brown of days earlier. Bursts of purple, white and yellow from crocuses, narcissi, and snowdrops popped everywhere—much to Mo's delight as she tromped alongside her mom. The sun had shed its wintery reserve and carried heat again, kissing every branch and bush with buds. Spring. It was usually a time of year Aisha loved, but today it kindled nostalgia and a strange longing, though for what exactly she couldn't say. (More like *won't admit*, her inner self snarked.)

She inhaled deeply. The cool, damp air smelled of fertile earth and the sharp sap of new growth. It should've been energizing and invigorating. Instead, it made her eyes tear.

Each sensory detail was as painful as catching yourself on a thorn in a blackberry patch, a reminder that just like the seasons did every year, whether you were prepared for them to or not, everything changed.

It was inevitable. And yet . . . could she seriously be considering leaving River's Sigh? Was she really willing to forsake tiny Minnow cabin, which had been her and baby Mo's refuge for all these impossibly sweet years? Then again, if someone had beaten her to the punch, was opening the very business she herself wanted to run, didn't she have to move? There wasn't room for two such similar shops in their small town.

Mo, Aisha's "baby," shuffled through a pile of twigs, smiling as they crunched under her boots and singing in the tinkly soprano of a little girl. *A little girl.* And that, in a nutshell, was why Aisha had the inevitability of change on her mind. As beloved as this place was and as much of a sanctuary as it had been for them, her "baby" was a *girl* now. And she, a kid when she'd birthed Mo, was a *woman.* River's Sigh was always supposed to be a temporary stay. A rock to rest on in the unexpected stream she'd found herself in. A safe spot to balance until she was ready to leap into the place she was actually supposed to be.

Four years ago, Aisha had been seventeen and facing an unplanned pregnancy under ugly circumstances, trying to decide if she should keep her baby or put her up for adoption like she herself had been, all while grieving the loss of her beloved mom. She never would've imagined that at twenty-one, she might feel just as confused as she had then.

She'd always considered twenty-anything, adult-*adult*, to be the age and stage of knowing . . . stuff.

Now she was hopeful that thirty would have more answers. It was a while to wait, of course, but it was good to have something to look forward to.

She'd expressed similar sentiments to her aunt the other day but hadn't exactly had them validated. Understatement. Jo was too kind to overtly squash her ideas about thirty, but Aisha caught a flash of suppressed laughter in her eyes. Knowing her luck, it meant Jo knew something she didn't—that she was fooling herself. Maybe you didn't know more at thirty than at twenty. Maybe all you learned, the older you got, was how much you still didn't know.

Mo's tiny hand clasped Aisha's. "Mom."

"Yes?"

But Mo's word wasn't a question. It was declarative. Like she wanted to inform Aisha, to remind her— or possibly to claim her, lest there was someone lurking around with any doubts—that Aisha was *her* mom. Or maybe she just wanted her cold little paws warmed up. Either way, it made Aisha smile, and she nodded at Mo. "Daughter."

Mo beamed and skipped along beside her, still holding her hand tightly.

As they continued down the trail, Aisha turned her thoughts to dinner. Something hearty and nourishing. Beef stew with roasted root vegetables, maybe? Mo especially loved turnips. Or Butternut squash lasagna? So creamy and good. As she'd learned so well from Jo, a home-cooked meal went a long way to soothing one's worries—and thinking about the task helped put her future in perspective, too.

Mo's hand in hers. Food to help her grow. A warm, snuggly bed. Clothes on her back. No matter how Aisha tended to obsess about things, what she had right now, in this moment, was all she really needed to know and focus on. She was a mom. A mother. It was a sacred gift and a calling, and she would live up to it.

She was grateful to Jo and Callum for letting them stay here, for enabling her to build a nest egg, for creating a sense of family and belonging, but it was time to figure out where she and Mo were supposed to put their own roots down long-term. Past time, actually.

Jo had hacked and coughed all last month. It was only a bad cold and she was mended now, plus Aisha was self-aware enough to realize the only reason it freaked her out was that since her mother died so young, she saw worst case scenarios everywhere. Still, it was a good nudge: being self-sufficient and reliant on no one had always been the goal, the plan. For the good of her child, she'd allowed herself to get waylaid, but it was time to make some tough decisions. To stay? To go? And either way, how to forge an independent life and permanent home for her and Mo, one that she was solely responsible for, one that no one but her had the power to build or tear down, one that was safe from all outside influences.

Chapter 2

THE GREYHOUND GROUND TO A halt and the bus driver's voice crackled over the speaker, announcing the stop. Greenridge. Jase was dozing and came to alertness slowly at first—then more quickly when he realized Colton no longer filled the seat beside him. One by one, the few people old-school enough, or broke enough, to still take a bus in this day and age filed off—but still no sign of Colton. Maybe he was in the john?

Jase unfolded his cramped limbs and lifted out of his seat, ducking his head to keep from knocking it on the overhead bins. A low voice purred behind him, "Offer still stands."

Rats. Becca. Still on the bus. He'd thought he was free and clear. He turned in the narrow aisle but didn't have to answer. Colton's grinning face appeared over Becca's shoulder, revealing where he'd disappeared to, though Jase should've known.

Colton spoke for Jase. "You're wasting your breath, sweetheart. Jase here is all work, no play."

Jase gave an apologetic one-shouldered shrug and

didn't disagree.

The diamond Monroe stud above the corner of Becca's heart-shaped mouth flashed in the dim overhead lights as she smiled. It was pretty if piercings were your thing, but they weren't his. Too impractical. Snagged on stuff. Ink was better. "If you change your mind, remember I put my number in your phone."

"Thanks." Jase smiled amiably, but thought, what kind of whack job grabs a random guy's phone and adds her name to his contacts? Ah, well, it took all sorts to make the world go around. Friendly Becca had boarded a few towns back and struck up conversation at a diner during a layover between bus transfers. She was fine but liked to party in ways he didn't. Colton, of course, had no such reservations.

Becca smoothed her short purple hair, waggled her fingers in farewell, then squeezed past him and swayed down the rubber-matted aisle, Colton stumbling behind her. Apparently, the party had already started.

Colton paused long enough to say, "I'll catch up with you tomorrow—meet you there, I mean."

Jase grimaced. All he needed was for Colton to show up for their first day of work hungover or worse, making them both look bad. Not a lot he could do about it though. His foster brother did what he wanted and only what he wanted and always had. Jase didn't fault him for it, but it wasn't how he was wired, no matter how often he wished it was.

He pulled his sweatshirt's hood up over his head,

hefted his backpack, which carried the full sum and total of his earthly belongings, including his steel-toed boots and climbers laced to one strap, then followed Colton and Becca's lead, hunching his shoulders to avoid hitting his head on the bus ceiling. When he stepped down onto the gravel shoulder, only a few of the other freshly debarked passengers openly stared, but all gave him a wide berth. It was the one perk of being freakishly large; strangers tended to be wary and steered clear. His shaved head, dark clothing, and heavy boots probably added to people's misconceptions, but he didn't cultivate an intimidating look on purpose. He was just practical. Long hair was hard to keep clean when you were on the road, and black clothes didn't show dirt.

Becca and Colton climbed into a jacked up truck sporting lots of chrome and a light bar that could probably be seen from Mars. The instant the passenger door slammed shut, the vehicle roared off in a belch of diesel fumes. Jase watched as one-by-one, other passengers disappeared into waiting vehicles—then surveyed his surroundings.

The stop was only saved from pitch-blackness by the glow of the strip lighting along the bus's side and a neon sign beaming "C-FFEE" from across the street.

Greenridge was new to Jase—well, new to both him and Colton, actually, but Colton hadn't discovered it, hadn't chosen it. He was just broke and decided, for practical reasons, to tag along when Jase came across the job listing online. It was more than that for Jase. It was an active decision. He was tired of city life and the constant partying Colton could never get enough of, and he liked small towns and had always wanted to explore the northwest. Admittedly though, this small and this far north might prove a bit much. The place seemed to have come together by accident, building up bit by bit alongside the highway and railway track that ran parallel to it.

Jase wondered if the town had once had a bus depot that closed down, a sign of changing times, or if Greenridge was so small it had never had an official one. Either way, being let off on the side of the highway in the middle of the night didn't do much to create a feeling of welcome.

"You're not here to be welcomed," he scoffed under his breath, since there was hardly anyone left to hear him. "You're here to make bank and take care of your responsibilities."

Tonight, however, alone in the dropping temperature, watching stranger after stranger take off with smiling friends and loved ones, Jase didn't feel as pragmatic as he tried to convince himself he was. He and Colton were only twenty-four, but he, at least, was starting to feel old—or like their lifestyle was.

Jase frowned. What was this mess in his head? He loved his nomadic life. Or found it the most comfortable way to live, anyway. If you're not attached to anything, you can't lose it and it can't be taken away.

He frowned deeper still.

He wasn't fooled by all the heartwarming greetings and tearful hugs of hello he'd just witnessed. For every happy reunion, somewhere nearby there was a huge fight brewing and a quick departure in the wings. For every mom or dad coming "home," there was another one leaving never to be seen again. And for every smiling lover, someone else was screaming and throwing things.

There were only two people left waiting now, a woman about his age with a small girl with pretty black braids. She reminded him so much of a picture he had of Emily from a few years back that he sucked in a breath. Did Emily still wear her hair like that or was it cut short or something? Familiar sadness and shame gut-punched him. What kind of loser didn't know that about his own kid? A beige Honda pulled up, slammed to a stop, and a man rushed out. "I'm so sorry I'm late, you guys."

"Daddy!" The little girl leaped into his arms. "I missed you!"

The adults laughed and as the guy hugged his daughter, the woman stepped into his embrace too.

The little scene was fresh salt in an old wound, reminding Jase that recounting all the miseries some folks faced was no true consolation. Of course, there were genuinely happy reunions and truly close-knit families. What would it be like to have a home to come back to? To have people who missed you when you went away, who celebrated when you returned? Jase had no idea. Never had.

As if shoved into motion by his thoughts, the bus groaned and grumbled its way back onto the road again, swinging wide into the empty lane and rolling on into the night. Jase watched the hostile red-rimmed eyes of its taillights until they disappeared. Then he checked both ways and crossed the highway. Small as it was, at least Greenridge had a 24-hour coffee shop.

As he walked, Jase patted the chest pocket of the jean jacket he wore over his hoodie, feeling for the reassuring fold of paper on the inside pocket. He'd read the ad so many times, he had it memorized. River's Sigh B & B—a pretty name to go with what would hopefully prove to be a nice place to bunk down for a while. And he'd already touched base. They were expecting him and Colton. And sure, it had been a while since either of them had fallen a tree—but it was a *bed and breakfast*. How wild of terrain could it be? The owners were looking for glorified landscapers and with his and Colton's letters of reference, they were in. He just hoped Colton would control his wild side and not ruin this opportunity for them.

Chapter 3

AISHA WALKED ALONG THE TRAIL from Silver cabin, carefully carrying the grungy bucket of mop water that she needed to dump, her mind wandering.

There'd been a slew of pre-arranged late checkouts today, so her cleaning schedule had been pushed back, but now, finally, each cabin was sparkling clean, perfectly restocked and prettily arranged again, ready for whoever its next guest might be.

She wasn't feeling the satisfaction she usually did at the end of a cleaning shift, however. The glow she got from a job well done had been dulled by time spent training two college students who were going to work for them April through August. The two girls were all right, she guessed, but they acted like every chore was drudgery or somehow beneath them—an attitude Aisha never understood. *No* job was beneath her.

It wasn't that she didn't feel frustration or annoyance when clients were slobs—and thankfully, most of their guests were awesome, so messes like today's were rare. It was that it was her job to clean it up and she took zealous pride in doing just that. Aisha had

expected similar enthusiasm, or at least similar dili-
gence, in the new hires and was disappointed. If they
didn't like scrubbing, didn't get a tiny thrill over a
gleaming toilet bowl, didn't derive a mild sense of
superiority from tidying other people's messes, why
did they even apply for housekeeping work? The north
was booming again. There were plenty of other places
hiring.

Then again, they were young. The thought triggered a wry smile because they were, no doubt, at least
her age if not older. Nevertheless, she'd take it as a
personal challenge to inspire them to be proud of their
work. And she'd try to stop taking it personally that Jo
and Callum were adding staff. It wasn't a sign they felt
Aisha couldn't handle everything. It was that River's
Sigh B & B was growing. It was exciting—and an
honor that she was in charge of new staff. She should
be celebrating.

Yes, *celebrating*. She was not a whiny, whinging
person. She didn't bitch and moan. She changed things
she was unhappy about. She would tackle—

Aisha's mini pep talk ended abruptly. Someone or
something was splashing ferociously in the creek
behind Rainbow cabin. There was a muffled grunt.
Then more splashing.

Her first thought was *bear*. Normally there was
enough action around the property—not to mention,
until recently, grizzled old Hoover barking his face off
at the slightest whiff of forest dwellers—that wildlife

stayed clear. But the season hadn't really started yet, and the grounds were extra quiet since Hoover passed, something Aisha tried to avoid thinking about because it filled her with so much sorrow for Jo who mourned him like the closest of personal friends, which, of course, he was.

And even in Hoover's day, barking maniac or not, it wasn't unheard of to have bear visitors this time of year. They always spotted at least a couple of black bears—and once a Kermode came through—in the spring, skinny and scrounging for easy food. Aisha wasn't scared exactly—no doubt it was just some hungry fella seeking dandelions and tender grass not available on the forest floor—but she wasn't an idiot either. A bear, if surprised, interrupted or made to feel threatened in any way, was a dangerous thing.

Moving more cautiously, she continued along the trail as it rounded the cabin—then slammed to a halt.

Two shirtless guys crowded the creek's scanty bank. One, incredibly massive with a shorn head and heavily tattooed back, was hunkered down, facing away from her. The other was . . . seriously hot. Wearing nothing but a well-worn pair of work jeans with suspenders dangling around his narrow hips, as if purposefully showing off his well-defined pecs and deeply cut six-pack, hell, *eight-pack,* of golden brown abs, and gleaming with droplets of creek water, he looked like he was modelling for some calendar featuring working men or something—not like he actually *was* a working man.

Wait—working man. Working *men*. Right. Aisha gave herself a mental facepalm. Jo and Callum had mentioned something about hiring some guys to fall dangerous trees around the property, do some of the heavier landscaping, and maybe even cut wood for the following winter.

She plunked the heavy mop bucket down. Filthy water sloshed over the rim, splashing her yoga pants with chemicals and stink. Awesome. She didn't quite manage to hold back a disgusted groan. The two men visibly jolted and turned in her direction. Seeing her, the tall guy—he really was a monster height-wise—looked even more startled, not less. And she realized that Hot Guy had hotter guy competition. He looked like Jason Momoa, if Jason Momoa had a shaved head.

Hot Guy was first to recover from the surprise. He gave her a quick once over, which Aisha hated but figured was fair enough considering her own gawking. Then he grinned and winked. Ugh.

"Um, this is a work place," she said, then winced. She'd intended to sound stern, but the comment came out like she was asking him, not telling him. Why was she having such a hard time stringing words together? Talking was her forte. And good grief. She'd seen half naked men before—even a fully naked man. Mo wasn't an immaculate conception—no matter how much Aisha wished otherwise.

Still, it had been a long while . . . or, more honestly, *never* since she'd seen guys—*men*—this good looking. She especially liked how the big guy didn't seem as cocky as Hot Guy who was already annoying her. He seemed shy and kept his head ducked, his eyes averted. . . .

Shit! Her hormones were making her stupid. This was another shift within her in recent months—maybe the most unwelcome of them all. For years now, it had been a relief, how totally not into guys she was. She'd gone on a few dates, even attended a three-day music festival with someone really nice—but it was like her brain, her body, her whole being had hung up a "Closed" sign. She hadn't felt the slightest spark of romantic interest in forever—certainly nothing strong enough to make her willing to risk emotional roller-coasters, potential headaches, or pain.

Then Mo turned four, and the sign flipped back to "Open." Completely against her will, Aisha transformed into a version of herself she hardly could accept as being *her*. A guy-obsessed weirdo. She saw men everywhere and was hyper-conscious of their presence—especially when they were in the middle of her usually private and safe woods, apparently.

Hot Guy laughed out loud, seeming to know exactly why she was uncomfortable. He stepped forward casually, thumbs hooked in his belt loops.

Just to avoid his brazen eyes, Aisha honed in on a felt-lined denim jacket and black sweatshirt that lay stacked on top of a big backpack, near a pair of heavy boots perched on a flat rock—a pair of boots so big they had to belong to the giant, who was still kneeling by the creek.

Like Hot Guy, Giant wore only a scruffy pair of low-slung jeans, giving Aisha an interesting-if-unexpected—and unwanted, she reminded herself— eyeful of his boxers and half his muscular butt.

He lumbered to his feet, and she realized he was well-muscled too, just his height camouflaged it a bit—stretching the muscle out over bone and sinew. His nipples were dark as plums against his light brown flesh which looked as firm as a wood plank. Said nipples were hard and erect, showing they felt the icy temperature of the creek water glistening on his skin, even if the rest of him didn't. Scrolling text adorned his rib cage, but she couldn't make out what it said from where she stood.

Unlike Hot Guy, he seemed uncomfortable at being caught washing up in the creek. His obvious discomfort made Aisha embarrassingly aware that she was staring, though she felt powerless to stop—until she caught herself following the line of fur that ran from his naval and disappeared into his waistband—

She gave herself another sharp mental slap. What was she doing?

The giant shifted uneasily and finally spoke. "I'm sorry. I, uh, was told the season hadn't started yet, that the place was empty."

Aisha's brow furrowed and she arched an eyebrow.

Who had told him that? And even if the place was empty, how did that explain the ice-water bath?

The stranger must've read the confusion on her face. He shook his head. "I'm Jason—call me Jase— Scott."

Was he kidding? His name was actually *Jason*? Nerves made her earlier inner comparison of him to the famous actor seem extra hilarious and she snort-giggled.

Jason—Jase—took another step back. She tried to rein herself in.

"And this is . . . my brother. Colton Hislop." He motioned at Hot Guy with a huge hand. "We're going to be working here? We've been on the road a while, so we wanted to, uh, freshen up before presenting ourselves?"

So she wasn't the only one afflicted with the awkward tendency to make statements into questions when nervous. The thought mollified her. "Well, too late for that. Consider yourself . . . presented."

Jase the giant blushed—or else he was finally feeling the chill. Either way, his tan skin definitely went rosy.

"Um, you're not . . . Jo, are you?" There was a soft, shy note in Jase's voice, as if he was pleading that she wasn't, but Aisha was distracted by Colton. He was pulling a soft gray Henley shirt over his head with what seemed to her an unnecessary amount of stretching and pausing.

A thunder bolt of irritation crashed through Aisha, way too large for such a tiny trigger, and she knew it.

"No, I'm not *Jo*, thank God," she snapped.

Jase's body quaked in a shiver. She guessed it was nice that he didn't want to "present" himself to Jo and Callum without cleaning up first, but what an insane place to do it. He couldn't rent a hotel room or something?

Still struck almost mute by the view, stupidly, humiliatingly, Aisha's face started to burn. Jase's height and size really were jaw-dropping. To her shame, she couldn't think of one witty line or sharp comment to mitigate her discomfort.

"Follow your brother's example and put on some clothes," she finally managed through gritted teeth. "This is a family establishment. Geez."

It was absolutely no consolation that Jase looked as uncomfortable as she felt as he obediently stooped over his pack and rummaged for a towel and a clean T-shirt.

Like she hadn't sounded dopey or bossy enough, she added, "You guys'll catch your death of pneumonia scrubbing up in a creek that had chunks of ice in it a week ago!"

She snatched up the mop bucket again and stalked off, knowing she looked—and sounded—like a complete looney. Put on some clothes? It wasn't like the guy was naked. And "family establishment?" True enough, sure, but what was her point, exactly? Plus, he was right. There was no one around. She was being a freak—and not in her usual good-freak sort of way.

Still, it wouldn't have been the worst exit, all said and done—except her stupid foot caught a root and threw her off balance. She managed, barely, to keep from falling, but upended the bucket in the process, drenching herself with the rest of the gloopy mess.

Behind her came a surprised, slightly dismayed grunt—and a low whistle, followed by laughter. Aisha didn't have to turn around to know Giant Jase was the grunter and his brother was the hyena. She resumed a forward march, without a backward glance. She might have to listen to them laugh at her, but she didn't have to watch.

To read on, catch your own copy of
THE CATCH today!

About the Author

 **Ev Bishop** is an award-winning author, who lives and writes in a remote small town in wildly beautiful British Columbia, Canada, a place that inspires the settings for her cozy contemporary romances.

In addition to writing novels, Ev was a long-time newspaper columnist with the *Terrace Standard* and is a prolific scribbler of articles, essays, short stories and poems.

www.ingramcontent.com/pod-product-compliance
Lightning Source LLC
Chambersburg PA
CBHW060222180626
46813CB00007B/2928